JOURNEY TO IMPOSSIBLE PLACES

BOOK 2·THE GREAT DIVIDE

TED DEKKER & H.R. HUTZEL

ISBN (Paperback Edition): 979-8-9865173-4-6

Also Available in the Journey to Impossible Places trilogy:

The Fall (Book One)
ISBN: 979-8-9865173-3-9 (Paperback Edition)

Redemption (Book Three)
ISBN: 979-8-9865173-5-3 (Paperback Edition)

Published by:

Scripturo
350 E. Royal Lane, Suite 150
Irving, TX 75039

Cover art and design by Manuel Preitano

Printed in the United States of America

CHAPTER ONE

CHARLIE SHIFTED BEHIND Brynn on the horse, unable to get comfortable in the saddle. They'd been traveling with hardly any stops for a day and a half toward the first stronghold. And though Charlie had some experience riding horses from his time at Mr. Abbott's ranch in Montana, he'd never been confined to one for this long. Brynn, on the other hand, didn't seem to mind. Neither did Talli, who switched between flying alongside them or riding atop the horse's head. Charlie shifted again and glanced up at the sky where the Roush now soared. Moonlight glimmered like silver on Talli's white wings.

Charlie shook his head, still unable to believe he'd accepted the mission to save the city of Lumina—or at least try to save it. *And* he was taking the journey with a girl he'd just met and a fluffy, talking batlike creature. If it didn't seem like a dream before, it sure did now.

Charlie mentally retraced the steps they'd taken so far, from the hillside cottage, where he met the Sage, down the mountainside to the desert they now trekked. Brynn had warned Charlie it would be a grueling ride, but Charlie underestimated just how challenging it would be. Their descent down the mountain had led them north, away from the House of Lumina and over a small but treacherous mountain range. Thankfully, the horse and Brynn seemed experienced with the rugged landscape.

At the lower altitude, the dense mountain pines had thinned and become sparser. The rocky earth had shifted to sand, and the cool mountain breeze warmed to something arid. The landscape was barren now, the trees few and far between, punctuated by lonely, scraggly bushes that looked like they hadn't had a drink for months. Charlie stared straight ahead at the bare horizon line, knowing that somewhere in the distance, a desert canyon would greet them. And inside that canyon would be the first stronghold.

Brynn shifted in front of him, as if sensing Charlie's angst growing with each passing minute. She unfolded their map and traced a finger across the parchment from the hillside cottage all the way to the first stronghold. "We're no more than two hours away," she said. "Do you want to try to catch some sleep before we get there? You can lean against me."

"Thanks," Charlie said, "but I'm way too nervous for that. Plus, I think my sleeping pattern is off from the constant darkness. I don't even feel tired."

"Well it *is* the middle of the day," she said. "But you hardly slept last night. I thought you might want to rest." She glanced back at him. "You doing okay?"

Charlie shrugged. "For someone who just learned they're a mystical portal world's last hope, well, I guess I'm doing about as well as can be expected."

"Don't forget the part about your mortal enemy being your twin brother," Brynn said. "Oh, and the part where your father slaughtered hundreds of innocent people."

"Right," Charlie said under his breath. "So hey, how do you tell the difference between day and night in Lumina? It all looks the same to me."

Charlie had watched the sky the entire time they'd traveled. It didn't seem to change. Wherever they went, regardless of how much time passed or how much the landscape shifted, the bright moon shone among a smattering of vibrant stars.

Talli, who'd been soaring above them, landed between the horse's ears and turned to face the two kids. "I want to hear this," he said. "It all looks the same to me too."

"It does? Huh." Brynn shrugged. "Well, the moon is brighter during the day. Have you noticed that?"

Charlie peered up at the moon. He wasn't sure he saw the difference. "Maybe. Is there anything else?"

Brynn nodded. "It's also warmer during the day."

Charlie paused, realizing several hours back when the temperature seemed to rise, he'd taken off the cloak the Sage had given him.

"And when it's warmer," Brynn continued, "the crickets chirp more. Listen." She paused. "Hear them?"

"Cool," Charlie said. "I definitely didn't notice that."

Talli shifted from foot to foot. "It's still so unusual, though." He shook his fluffy head. "The darkness is always present here. And I have a feeling it will only get darker on our journey."

Charlie watched the Roush from around Brynn's shoulder. Something in his words unsettled Charlie. He rolled his shoulders to shake off a shiver, then reached into the leather shoulder bag draped across Brynn's back. He pulled out an apple.

"Brynn, Talli, you hungry?"

Talli shook his head.

"I'll take something," Brynn said.

Charlie handed her the apple, then pulled out a piece of jerky for himself. He took a bite and swallowed. Feeling a wave of nerves wash over him, he tried to distract himself. "So where'd you learn how to ride?" he asked Brynn, while turning his gaze to the starry sky.

Brynn was silent a moment before saying, "My parents used to have horses. How about you?"

The mention of Brynn's parents reminded Charlie of the solarflies she'd told him about back at the cottage. And for the first time Charlie realized he hadn't seen any glowing butterflies since arriving in Lumina. "I learned back at the orphanage where I used to live," he said.

"What was it like growing up there?" she asked.

"Well, I was only there for three months," he said. "But it was awesome. I was hoping to get adopted by Mr. Abbott, but—"

Charlie hesitated. When he'd paused too long, Brynn turned to look at him. "What's wrong?" she asked.

"Nothing," Charlie said. "It just feels like that was a lifetime ago. So much has happened since then. My whole life is different."

"I think I know what you mean," Brynn said. "I had a similar experience when my parents passed. I felt like I wasn't the same person anymore. Everything in my life had changed. And when your life changes that much, *you* have to change too."

Charlie considered her words. "Have to?"

"Yeah," she said. "You're going to change anyway. That's what happens when your life flips upside down.

The important thing is to choose *how* you want to change, so the person you become is better than the person you were before."

"Or," Talli said, "instead of changing into someone different, you could choose to become the person you've always been but didn't realize you were."

Both Charlie and Brynn gave him a quizzical look. Talli shrugged and turned around to face the front.

They waited for an explanation. When Talli didn't offer one, Charlie asked Brynn, "So you grew up with the constant darkness?"

She nodded. "I did. My parents were just young kids on the Day of the Turning. Or at least, that's the story my mom told me."

"The Day of the Turning?" Charlie said. "Is that what you call it? The day the Sovereign—I mean, my father—brought the darkness to Lumina?"

She nodded. "When I was little, my mom said a light used to fill the sky. It was even brighter than the moon. But on the Day of the Turning, a black cloud snuffed out the light and overtook the land. She said it rolled in like a fog, but it was violent—it shook the ground and rattled the spice jars on the shelves."

Charlie furrowed his brow. "I thought the Sage said no one in Lumina remembered the Light of the World?"

Brynn turned in the saddle to look at him. "What's the Light of the World?" she asked.

Talli spun back to them, his green eyes wide with excitement. "Where I come from," he said, "the Light of the World is a person. Actually, more than one person. Because he who was the Light of the World made a great sacrifice so others would know they, too, are the Light of the World."

Brynn glanced at Charlie with a confused look then back at Talli. "You know," she said to the Roush, "not much of what you say makes sense."

"Perhaps it is your ears that don't make sense," Talli said with a slight smirk. Before Brynn could respond, he turned to Charlie. "What's the Light of the World where you come from?" he asked.

Charlie shrugged, then said, "Just a story."

"Hmmm," Talli said. "It seems in both of your worlds the Light has become a legend. But that's okay." he said. "Just because something's a legend doesn't mean it isn't true. Oh look!" Talli pointed with his wing. "I think we've arrived."

A black line, even darker than the normal darkness, spread across the horizon.

Brynn ushered the horse forward.

A canyon expanded in front of them, seeming to swallow all light.

When they reached the edge, Brynn stopped the horse. The kids dismounted, and Talli took to the sky. Charlie watched as the white Roush flapped his wings and glided over the vast canyon. He swooped low, down into the ravine, over a small circle of trees in the center, then back up to meet the children. He landed on the edge.

Charlie couldn't take his eyes off the strange circular oasis of greenery in the center of the valley. A shiver worked its way through his shoulders, then slithered down his spine.

"Is that the stronghold?" Charlie asked.

"It appears so," Talli said. "The two of you will need to hike down. I suggest leaving the horse. The path seems too steep and narrow." He stretched out his wings. "I'll fly. My footsteps are wobbly enough on flat ground."

"I'll tie up the horse," Brynn said. She grabbed the reins, led the creature to a large desert bush, and secured its lead. She rubbed the horse's forehead, then returned to Charlie, who was still staring over the canyon's edge.

"You ready?" she asked in a low whisper.

"No," Charlie said. "But I'll do it."

He walked along the rim until he found a trailhead that would lead them down into the basin of the gorge. Talli was right, the path was narrow and incredibly steep.

Brynn took the lead, demonstrating short shuffling

steps. It took them fifteen long minutes to painstakingly wind their way down the east side of the canyon and reach the bottom. Talli stayed close but remained in the air.

Brynn reached the bottom several feet ahead of Charlie. She traipsed across the barren ground toward their destination—the small circular grove of trees that waited like an oasis.

The piercing light of the moon illuminated Brynn's red hair, and Charlie couldn't help but wish that she could enter the stronghold. Not him. Brynn looked confident, her long strides strong and purposeful. She held her shoulders back and her head high. She was a year younger than Charlie, but to him, she seemed much older, more capable. If one of them was equipped to enter the stronghold, it was her.

Brynn bounced backward as if hitting an invisible wall.

She froze, hands grasping the sides of her head. Then she crumpled into a ball on the ground.

"Brynn!" Charlie rushed to her side. "Are you okay? What happened?"

She was still doubled over, head in her hands. She moaned something incoherent.

Talli flapped down from the sky and landed beside them. "What happened?" he asked. "Is she hurt?"

"I don't know." Charlie said. He placed a hand on Brynn's back. She breathed heavily.

"Brynn?" he said again. "What happened?"

Brynn drew a deep breath and slowly unfolded her body. She leaned on Charlie, then stood upright on shaky legs. Her milky-gray eyes appeared even more clouded than normal. "Don't you feel that?" she asked Charlie in a breathless voice. Her hands clutched the sides of her head again. She fell to her knees. "Ahhh!" she screamed.

"What's happening to you?" Charlie shouted.

"My head feels like it's going to explode." She groaned. "There's a loud pulsing in my ears. It hurts, and I'm dizzy."

Talli placed a wing on her shoulder. "It must be the stronghold," he said, then pointed toward the trees about a hundred yards away.

Charlie took a step toward it. Then another.

Then he felt it.

A subtle vibration pulsed, not just in his head, but throughout his body.

He turned back to Talli and Brynn. "I think you're right," he said. "The Sage said Brynn can't enter the strongholds. This must be why."

"You can feel it?" Talli asked Charlie.

Charlie nodded.

Talli's green eyes widened. "What does it feel like?"

Charlie shook his head. "I don't know how to describe it. It's like an ominous pulse or something."

Brynn glanced up at him. "No, Charlie. It feels like pure darkness."

A chill raced down Charlie's spine.

"I think we should get her farther back from the stronghold," Talli said.

"Good idea."

Charlie and Talli helped Brynn return to the bottom of the trail, several yards back from the spot where she first felt the stronghold's effects.

"How are you feeling?" Charlie asked her. "Any better?"

Brynn nodded and removed the canteen from her belt. She took a big swig of water. "I think I'll be okay." She panted. "But Charlie, what about you?"

Charlie pressed his lips together. "What about me?"

"Are you really going in there?" She glanced at the stronghold. "I mean, I wanted to go on this mission with you. I wanted to help you save Lumina. But I'm not so sure now."

Charlie hesitated, then looked to Talli.

"The choice is still yours, young Charlie. Whether you stay or go is up to you. But I'm afraid I must stay." Talli gestured to Brynn. "I don't think I should leave her."

"No!" Brynn said. "You have to go with Charlie! You can't let him go in there alone!"

"But he won't be alone," Talli said. "He's never alone."

Talli's words stirred Charlie's memory, reminding him of something the Sage had said before they left.

Charlie glanced at Brynn. Just moments ago, he'd admired her strength and confidence. If someone like Brynn couldn't survive the stronghold, he wondered how he ever would.

"I'll go," Charlie finally said. "I have to. This is why we came."

A smile spread across Talli face.

A look of terror formed on Brynn's. "Be careful," she said to Charlie. "And remember, it's the Stronghold of Envy."

"Right," Charlie said. He paused then added, "Wish me luck?"

Brynn stared at him, then said, "You're going to need more than luck in there."

Talli draped a wing over Brynn's shoulders but looked to Charlie. "You *will* need more than luck," he said. "But the good news is, everything you need is already inside you."

"That's what the Sage said," Charlie whispered to himself.

But he still would have liked some luck.

Chapter One

Charlie's chest rose as he drew a big shaky breath. He turned toward the stronghold, then took a step forward. Then another. With every step, the thrum grew louder in his ears. The pulse in his body intensified. And so did the thought that Charlie might be making the biggest mistake of his life.

CHAPTER TWO

SARAH PACED BACK and forth on the island's beach, watching Tyler pull himself out of the waves and onto the shore. Becca confronted him immediately.

"Well?" she asked him. "Did you see it? Was there any sign of the plane?"

Tyler held up a hand while he caught his breath. The rest of the group circled him now. Even Sarah made her approach to hear what he had to say.

"There's nothing out there." Tyler panted.

"Nothing?" Becca's voice was shrill. "You didn't see anything? Anywhere?"

Tyler wiped the water from his face and met Becca's frantic stare. "No, Becca. I didn't see anything. But I only searched the area where the plane used to be. I can't search the entire ocean."

"Right," Becca said, lowering her voice.

"No wreckage of any kind?" Kurtis asked.

Tyler shook his head, then gestured to Milo. "It's like Milo said. It's as if the plane disappeared."

"With Charlie and Michael and the rest of our stuff?" Fear tinted Maxine's voice.

"So what do we do now?" Raegan asked, arms hugging her waist.

Becca cleared her throat and straightened her shoulders. "We take action," she said. Sarah could hear the subtle quiver in Becca's voice, but she hid her fear well. "We need to set up a new camp," Becca said. "What all do we need? Food, shelter, firewood …"

"A way off this island," Tyler said.

"And we need to find Charlie and Michael," Sarah added. "Something isn't right here."

Tyler's eyes found hers. Sarah couldn't read his face, but she didn't need to in order to know what he was thinking. He'd already made that clear. Tyler believed Charlie had hurt Michael, and Sarah was somehow involved.

Sarah ignored him. "I'll volunteer to gather food," she said, raising her hand. It would give her the opportunity to continue searching for Charlie as well. The plane may have disappeared, but Sarah knew Charlie was still somewhere on the island.

"I'll go with you," Maxine said, taking a step closer to Sarah.

"I'll join as well," Kurtis said.

"Great," Becca said. She folded her arms across her chest. "So that takes care of food."

"There's a rocky overhang down the beach," Joey said timidly. "It's not a cave, but it should keep us dry."

"Perfect," Becca said. "So shelter is covered. We still need firewood, though. Tyler, will you do that?"

Tyler shook his head. "Sorry. I can't. I have more important things to take care of."

"Such as?"

"Such as finding whoever took our stuff." Tyler looked to Kurtis. "Kurtis said it's the most logical explanation for the disappearance of our supplies. And I agree." Tyler's eyes darted to Sarah. "I think we need to stick to logical explanations for now."

Sarah clenched her jaw.

"I'm going with Tyler," Raegan said.

Milo raised his hand. "Me too."

"I don't think this is a practical use of our time," Becca said. "Our food and supplies were probably washed out with the tide. And you guys already searched the island once and said there's no one else here. Not to mention we covered the entire island today while searching for Michael and Charlie. If other people were here, we'd have seen them by now."

"Just like we would have seen Michael and Charlie?"

Tyler asked. He shook his head. "No. I'll agree with Sarah on one thing: something isn't adding up here. And I'm going to figure out what it is. Besides, Becca, all we have is time. Remember? No one's coming for us now. The transponder is gone."

Sarah swallowed. Tyler had a point.

Becca seemed to come around to his idea as well, because she huffed and said, "Fine. See what you can find. But be careful. And bring back whatever food you can carry. We don't have the backpacks anymore, so we'll have to get creative."

"I've got that covered!" Milo said and pulled his shirt off over his head. Sarah watched him tie the sleeves together, then loop it around his shoulder.

She glanced down at her uniform blazer still tied around her waist. It looked like Sarah had the ability to get creative too—at least when it came to collecting food.

But what Sarah couldn't figure out was how in the world she was going to get creative enough to find her best friend when it seemed like he'd disappeared—and creative enough to convince Tyler that both she and Charlie were innocent.

The late-afternoon sun sat low in the sky and filtered

through the dense jungle trees at an odd angle. As Sarah trudged along, she adjusted the satchel she'd made from her blazer and hung around her shoulders. Maxine and Kurtis were close behind her. So far, they hadn't found anything—no food and still no sign of Charlie or Michael.

Sarah's stomach growled with hunger.

"It's like all the food disappeared too," Maxine said.

Sarah turned and looked back at the girl. "We'll find something," she said. She didn't dare mention she'd been fearing the same thing. Their situation was becoming more dire and stranger by the minute, and Sarah couldn't shake the thought that there was something very wrong with this island.

Sarah glanced back over her shoulder, noticing that Kurtis had fallen behind. He stopped to examine a plant, then stooped to check the soil. Sarah wondered if he was looking for clues to locate Charlie and Michael or just satisfying his own curiosity. How Kurtis could think about anything other than getting off the island, Sarah couldn't understand. Then again, her mind was completely occupied with concerns for Charlie. So much so, she almost didn't see the banana tree up ahead. Yellowish-green fruit hung from its branches.

"Thank goodness," Sarah sighed. She called back to Kurtis. "Hey, there's some bananas up here."

"Be right there," Kurtis said.

Maxine stopped beside Sarah. Fortunately, she'd worn a light windbreaker jacket on the plane and still had it. Sarah showed her how to tie the sleeves together to make a carrying pouch, then started to pull bananas off the tree. She handed them to Maxine.

"What's that?" Maxine asked and pointed.

"What's what?" Sarah followed the direction of her finger.

Maxine pointed to a thinning spot in the tree line. "It's like a clearing or something," Maxine said.

Sarah placed a banana into her blazer, then ducked her head to get a better view through the branches. She took a step forward. "I don't know. I can't tell from here. Let's go see what it is."

Maxine followed Sarah through the foliage until it thinned. Together they entered a semicircular clearing. Sarah stopped at the edge, speechless. A moment later, Kurtis joined them.

"Whoa," Kurtis said.

Sarah watched him remove his broken glasses then clean the lenses with the hem of his T-shirt. He returned them to his face, then took a step into the clearing.

"I don't remember this," Maxine said.

"Me either." Sarah's eyes scanned the open space and landed on the massive black tree that grew like gnarled roots up the side of a cliff. The tree's bark was as black as night.

"I don't think we've been to this part of the island before," Sarah said.

Kurtis turned to look at her. "We haven't. I'd remember this because I've never seen a tree like that in all my life—in person or in a picture."

"What kind of tree is it?" Maxine asked.

Kurtis took a step toward it. "That's just it," he said. "I don't know."

Sarah glanced at him. "How's it possible we missed this?" she asked. "The island is small. We should have seen this before, right?"

Kurtis nodded. "I don't know how we missed it. Maybe someone else from our group has seen it before." He looked up at the sky and spun in a slow circle to examine their surroundings. "We're in the center of the island. I crossed through this way yesterday when I was gathering food with Michael, Charlie, and the others."

Sarah shifted at the mention of her best friend.

"Let's go check out the tree," Kurtis said. He stepped into the clearing, and Sarah and Maxine followed.

The tree towered over the three kids as they stood beneath its leafless, rootlike branches. Kurtis walked around to the left side while Maxine followed Sarah around to the right.

Sarah's gaze traced the smooth black bark. "Watch your step, Maxine," she said, pointing to a root that protruded from the ground.

Maxine didn't respond but carefully picked her way over the thick roots that lined the earth like blood vessels. The massive tree clearly needed the large root system to support its sprawling canopy of branches. Some of its limbs hung so low, Sarah had to duck underneath them, while its tallest branches reached even higher than the cliff.

"Is the tree dead?" Maxine asked in a near whisper.

"I don't know," Sarah said, her voice also low. "It doesn't have any leaves." She took a step closer. Sarah wasn't sure why, but there was something about this tree that made her feel like she had to approach it quietly.

Maxine continued around the side of the trunk to the place where the tree met the cliff's face.

Sarah kept Maxine in sight but lingered between a section of drooping branches. They surrounded her like a cage, and Sarah couldn't explain why, but the embrace comforted her. Since the moment they'd crashed on the island, Sarah had felt lost and adrift. Her only solace in this horrifying experience had been Charlie. And now he was gone.

Sarah felt tears well in her eyes.

Had Charlie run away because of their fight?

A hot tear trickled down her cheek as Sarah finally allowed herself to consider that she might be the reason for Charlie's disappearance. Another tear quickly followed the first as the weightiness of her situation hit her afresh.

Sarah was lost on an island with no way off and no way to communicate with the world outside. Her friends were quickly falling apart under the weight of this realization as well. And worst of all, two members of their group were missing— including her best friend.

Sarah glanced up at the sky and blinked back tears. The late afternoon sun was shielded by the cliffside, but its warm rays crept over the edge and highlighted the branches of the tree with a red golden glow. Sarah wiped her eyes, then squinted, catching another spark distinct from the warm sunlight—a subtle yellow flicker in one of the low branches. Sarah stood on her tiptoes.

A cocoon hung from the branch of the tree above her head. The silklike chrysalis was two inches long and translucent enough that Sarah could see what looked to be a tiny glowing caterpillar inside the thin casing. Its light seemed to flicker as the creature twisted and turned.

More tears flooded Sarah's eyes, but this time, they

were tears of joy. This cocoon was the ounce of hope she needed—a reminder of her friend and the glowing butterflies he claimed to see. And perhaps a sign that everything was going to be okay.

Carefully, Sarah removed the cocoon from the branch. She pulled out the empty water bottle that had been in her pocket and gently tucked the silk-wrapped caterpillar inside the small plastic container.

"Hey guys, over here." Kurtis called. "I found some mangos and nuts."

Sarah slipped the water bottle into her pocket, careful not to squish it, then turned to Maxine. She was a few yards away in the crevice between the tree and cliff, hand raised to touch the smooth surface of the rock.

"Maxine, let's go," Sarah said.

Maxine froze, her hand in the air. She dropped it, then followed Sarah around the other side of the tree. Kurtis's arms were filled with mangos and another fruit Sarah didn't recognize.

"These are from a Malabar chestnut tree," Kurtis said. He dropped one of the palm-sized green pods onto the ground and stomped it with his shoe. The hard casing split, and he held it up for Sarah and Maxine to see. "There are nuts inside." He pulled one out to show them. "They'll add some protein and fat to our diets."

He handed the nut to Sarah, then popped another one into his mouth. Sarah tried the one he'd given her. It tasted like a peanut, and after days of only bananas and mangos, it tasted like the best peanut she'd ever had.

Sarah removed her blazer from her shoulders and began filling the makeshift pouch with as many nut pods as she could carry. She smiled, thinking about the cocoon tucked inside her pocket. Already things were looking up.

Tyler traipsed through the jungle with Raegan and Milo close in tow. Sweat beaded his brow; his body ached with exhaustion, but he didn't slow his pace. He wouldn't let Raegan and Milo see him tired. He couldn't allow a crack to form in the tough facade he'd created for himself—not now. But the truth was, along with being exhausted and confused, Tyler was terrified.

How had their supplies disappeared?

Where had the plane gone? He'd searched as far and as deep as he could swim, and he found no sign of it or anything from the beach.

And more importantly, what in the world had happened to Michael and Charlie?

Just days ago, Tyler never would have thought Charlie had it in him to hurt Michael—or anyone for that matter. In fact, he never thought he'd see Michael use physical force either. Sure, Michael was hard on Charlie. He harassed him and teased him. Some might even call it bullying. And yes, Tyler had participated in the fun. But that's all it was supposed to be—fun.

Or so Tyler had thought.

But the way Michael and Charlie had looked at each other on that cliffside had terrified Tyler almost as much as the plane crash. For the first time in his life, he'd seen two human beings with murderous intentions written on their faces.

Worse, Tyler felt rage clouding his own mind.

He knew Sarah was hiding information about Michael and Charlie's whereabouts. And the only logical conclusion he could make as to *why* she would do that was because something terrible happened to Michael at Charlie's hand. Sarah was trying to cover it up long enough for them to get rescued.

Tyler had suspected the two of them were up to no good when he saw Sarah chase Charlie down the beach the evening that Charlie and Michael had their fight on the cliff. Sarah had been distant ever since. Then, later that night, Charlie and Michael had disappeared together into the forest. Or at least, that's what Milo had said. None of it made sense to Tyler—until they'd found a scrap of Michael's bloodied shirt.

A wave of fear washed over him. It was the same feeling Tyler had experienced when the plane plummeted toward the sea. The same feeling he now felt every time he thought of his best friend, who was lost, hurt, or worse.

Tyler had been there to protect Michael on the cliff, but this time he'd failed his friend.

Guilt plagued him. He shoved the thoughts from his head and pushed forward, scanning the jungle for any sign of people who existed there besides their group of ten.

Milo had called them *others*, saying that's what the mysterious island people were called on the TV show *Lost*.

Tyler wished he'd quit talking about the show. Milo's theories about the island were starting to freak him out.

He and Milo both agreed on one thing, though. Other people had to be on the island. Nothing else made sense.

Unless Milo's crazy theories were true, and the island had some mystical powers …

Tyler shook his head. His thoughts spiraled. It seemed as if his mind became more clouded and confused with every minute he spent on this island.

"Hey, you okay?" It was Raegan. She walked beside him, her face dirty with sweat and soil, her damp hair pulled back into a ponytail.

Tyler straightened his shoulders. "I'm fine. Just thinking about what I'm going to do once we find the people who took our stuff."

He saw her glance at him out of the corner of her eye. "Do you think they'll be"—she hesitated—"I don't know, friendly?"

"Friendly?" Tyler turned to look at her. Raegan was a total tomboy and usually made herself out to be as tough as him. She was two years younger than Tyler and his constant shadow since she arrived at the orphanage. But today, he saw the fear in her eyes. "No. I don't think they're going to be friendly," Tyler said. "But that's okay because I don't plan to be friendly with them either."

"Me either!" Milo dropped down in between Tyler and Raegan from a tree branch directly overhead.

Raegan shrieked. "Don't do that!" She smacked Milo on the arm.

Tyler composed himself, trying not to let Raegan see that he, too, was startled.

"Hey!" Milo swatted back at her. "I'm working on my surprise attack. Looks like it worked."

Raegan rolled her eyes. "What's on your face?"

Tyler noted the smears of mud Milo wore in lines

and dots across his cheeks and forehead.

"War paint, of course." Milo shrugged.

Raegan made a disgusted face, then walked ahead.

"What's her problem?" Milo asked.

Tyler shook his head.

"Hey, come here." Raegan called back. "I found something."

Tyler motioned for Milo to follow him.

"Look at this," Raegan said when they reached her.

The trees had thinned and the shoreline of the backside of the island was visible from where they stood. Tyler followed the point of Raegan's finger. Off to the right, just a few yards away, a triangular rock formation jutted from the earth. Tyler scanned the mountainlike feature with his eyes, guessing it had to be at least a hundred feet tall. The sight of the giant rock was unsettling. It took Tyler several seconds to figure out why it bothered him. Then it clicked.

Tyler was almost certain he'd stood in this exact spot on the island once before, and this rock hadn't been here. It was as if it had sprung up from the ground, like the island was changing …

More likely, Tyler was losing his mind.

The late afternoon light cast strange shadows over the rock's uneven surface, giving the appearance of a face in the stone.

Tyler rolled his shoulder to shake off a shiver.

"There's fruit," Raegan said, pointing.

That's when Tyler noticed the emerald-green vines that snaked their way down the side of the jagged structure. Glossy eggplant-colored fruit mingled with the tiny leaves.

Tyler crossed the short distance to the sloping stone wall. The air was thick with a sweet smell. The vining plant cascaded from the top of the rock all the way down to its base.

Tyler reached out and plucked a piece of fruit off the vine.

"What are they?" Milo asked.

Tyler examined the fist-sized oblong fruit. "Plums?" he said.

"I don't think those are plums." Raegan was beside him, staring at the fruit in his hand.

"What if they're poison plums?" Milo asked.

Tyler shot him a look. "It's a regular plum. See?" Tyler dug his fingernails into the fruit's soft flesh and pulled it apart. The inside was lavender-purple, and the pit in the center was blood-red.

"Definitely not a plum," Raegan said. "Maybe Milo's right. We shouldn't eat that."

Sticky juice from the separated fruit dripped down Tyler's fingers. The scent was unlike anything he'd ever smelled. His mouth watered, and suddenly, all Tyler could think about was eating the fruit. His concerns about Michael faded. His fears about getting off the island vanished.

The sound of Tyler's own heartbeat thrummed in his ears. A sensation like ravenous hunger washed over him. It was the most intense craving he'd ever had. And somehow Tyler knew only this fruit would satisfy it.

A soft pulsing sensation formed in his palm. Tyler couldn't tell if it was from the fruit or the feel of his own blood coursing through his veins.

He lowered his face to the fruit to examine it closer. Tiny juice-filled sacks, similar to an orange, glistened in the late afternoon sunlight. The scent intensified.

"It smells like …" Tyler couldn't put his finger on it, but it was familiar. He held the fruit right under his nose and drew a deep breath, then he bit into the juicy flesh.

Flavor flooded Tyler's mouth. Sweetness exploded on his tongue. He closed his eyes and savored the bite, then ate the fruit to the pit.

When he opened his eyes, Raegan and Milo were staring at him.

"Well?" Raegan asked.

Tyler chuckled. "Well, it's definitely not a plum." He pulled another one off the vine and took a big bite out of its flesh. Juice ran down his chin. "It's the best thing I've ever eaten."

Raegan eyed him suspiciously.

Without hesitation, Milo grabbed one for himself. "Whoa," he said with his mouth full.

Tyler watched an expression of pure delight wash over Milo's face.

Raegan didn't wait any longer to try one. "It tastes like strawberry shortcake!"

"Mine tastes like cotton candy!" Milo said.

Tyler had been thinking it reminded him of his favorite chocolate-cherry ice cream. Aloud he said, "It tastes like heaven."

"Hand me another one, Milo," Raegan demanded.

Milo had one in each hand. He shook his head and quickly took a bite from each one as if to claim them.

Tyler laughed, then picked another piece of fruit for both him and Raegan.

She didn't even thank him before taking a big bite. "Look!" She pointed. "There's tons of them!"

She was right. The glossy green vines seemed to cover even more of the stone structure than they had moments ago. There were dozens, even hundreds of the fist-sized purple fruits.

"Dude, your lips are purple." Milo pointed at Tyler's mouth, then stuck out his tongue. "How about me?"

Raegan started giggling hysterically when Milo revealed the swirls of purple on his tongue.

Tyler felt a ripple of laughter bubble up within him. He let it out. It felt good to laugh with his friends again.

But beneath his glee, another sensation coursed through his body—a thrum like the one he'd felt in his fingers when he'd first held the fruit. Now it pulsed through his veins, flooding his entire body with a tingling chill. It awakened his mind and cleared away the confusion. He couldn't explain it, but he felt as if he understood the island now—as if it spoke to him.

Hello, Tyler. I've been waiting for you.

The thought echoed in his mind like a distinct voice. And the more he ate the fruit, the louder the voice became.

So Tyler ate more.

And more.

And he knew, no matter how much he ate, it would never be enough.

CHAPTER THREE

CHARLIE SWALLOWED against the tightness in his throat, unsure if it was from the dry desert air that filled the canyon or the fear of entering the Stronghold of Envy. Moonlight glimmered off the towering trees that formed the dense circle of forest. Charlie shook off a shiver, thinking the stronghold looked like an island in a dried-up ocean. The thought stirred memories of the island where he'd crashed.

Charlie wondered what Sarah was doing now, wondered if she'd noticed he was gone. And if she did know, did she even care? After the way Charlie had left things with her, he wouldn't blame her if she didn't.

He shoved the thoughts away and drew a deep breath, mustering every ounce of strength and courage he had. He crossed the last few feet of desert before the thick perimeter of trees. Then he entered the stronghold.

The atmosphere immediately changed. Cool air, fragrant with the scent of wet earth, rushed over Charlie. Before him, a path stretched out through the center of the trees. Not knowing where else to go or what to do, Charlie decided to follow it.

The ground was level and damp, the path straight. Thick forest lined both sides of the trail as far as Charlie could see. Vines with tiny yellow flowers draped from the canopy, mingling with the Spanish moss that clung to the branches.

The stronghold was surprisingly beautiful and not at all what Charlie had expected for a cursed fortress created by the most evil man in Lumina. Charlie shivered, the splendor somehow making the stronghold more unsettling.

A soft mist rolled across the ground, forming a dark fog around Charlie's feet. It parted as he made his way down the path, reminding Charlie of the story Brynn had told him about the black cloud that shrouded the light of Lumina on the Day of the Turning.

After nearly ten minutes of walking, Charlie noticed a shaft of light ahead on the path. It poured down from the canopy and illuminated a small structure. Charlie quickened his pace, and the scene came into view.

The thick oaklike trees parted to form a round clearing. Moonlight highlighted a gazebo at the center.

Pristine white pillars surrounded the platform.

Charlie approached the gazebo with breath held. His booted feet padded softly on the dirt, then squeaked against the first marble step. He climbed the second, third, and fourth, then stepped onto the bright-white floor.

A waist-high pillar was situated in the center of the platform, and an amber-colored orb floated above it, pulsing with a soft glow. Charlie glanced around before approaching, feeling the sinister vibration of the stronghold in his body as he neared it. He stopped directly in front of the amber orb. It was about the size of a basketball and encased a sapphire-blue, diamond-shaped stone.

"The key," Charlie whispered. He peered through gaps in the columns to the surrounding trees. "But that was too easy," he said to himself.

The Sage had told Charlie he'd have to face his deepest darkness to overcome each stronghold.

He stood in Stronghold of Envy. "Maybe I don't have any envy to overcome," Charlie said.

He reached out with a cautious hand to touch the amber orb. It was solid, like resin. He placed his palm flat on the surface, wondering if his hand would magically pass through its exterior. But nothing happened.

Charlie tapped his knuckles on the orb's surface.

Again, nothing.

He tried to remove it from its floating position above the pillar pedestal, groaning as he struggled. "If I could just drop it and break it …" he said.

But the orb didn't budge.

Maybe he could crack it. Frustrated, Charlie turned to look for a rock, then froze.

A door stood behind him on the dirt path he'd just traveled.

It hadn't been there before.

Charlie stiffened, then descended the stairs.

The door was simple, made of plain wood with a full-length mirror mounted to its flat surface. Moonlight shimmered on the glass. Charlie crossed the short distance between him and the door, coming face-to-face with something he hadn't seen in days—his own reflection.

Charlie hesitated in front of the image, taken aback by what he saw. Dressed in clothes that weren't his own, Charlie barely recognized himself. His usually close-cropped curly hair was longer than normal and frizzy on the ends, and his brown skin appeared even darker in this perpetual nighttime world. The golden-brown eyes of Charlie's reflection met his. He scanned himself from head to toe. He'd forgotten how small and weak he really looked. The Sage had convinced Charlie he was well-equipped for this mission. But now, after seeing himself, Charlie wasn't so sure.

He ran a hand over his hair to try to smooth his curls. A familiar feeling of insecurity washed over him as he remembered another recent time he stood in front of a mirror.

He pictured Michael entering the bathroom behind him. Imagined Tyler stacking his elbow on top of Charlie's head, commenting on how small he was. He smelled the scent of the red permanent marker that Michael had used to draw on Charlie's shirt.

"*F* is for *failure*," Michael had said.

For a moment, Charlie lingered on the memory, then he pushed it away.

He reached out a hesitant hand, wrapping his fingers around the doorknob in front of him. He twisted and pushed.

The door groaned open.

Charlie peered inside, expecting to see something. *Anything.*

Instead, he was greeted with nothing.

The door opened to reveal the path that stretched back toward the way he'd entered the stronghold. He stuck his head through, just to be sure, even stepped across the threshold to see if it was a portal, like back on the island. But nothing happened.

Charlie raised his eyebrows then shook his head.

"Okay. That was weird." He closed the door and turned back to the gazebo.

The doorknob rattled behind him.

Charlie spun, seeing the doorknob twist and the door crack open.

He took a step back. Ice filled his veins.

The door swung wide. And Tyler stepped through.

Charlie took another step back.

"Hey, Charlie," Tyler said with a sneer. He leaned against the doorframe. "Did you miss me?"

Charlie blinked. "What are you doing here?" he asked. He couldn't hide the surprise from his voice.

"I'm here to help you get that key," Tyler said, gesturing toward the gazebo. "Because we both know you're too weak to get it yourself."

Charlie shook his head. "You can't be here. You're on the island."

"Does it look like I'm on the island?" Tyler asked.

He sauntered through the door, closed it behind him, then circled Charlie as a predator might. Tyler stopped behind him. "Wow. Look at you." Tyler pointed to Charlie's reflection in the mirror, then pushed Charlie closer to the door. Together they stared at the image. "Man." Tyler shook his head. "You look terrible, Charlie. Really. Even more terrible than usual."

Charlie stiffened. His heart pounded in his ears.

Tyler grabbed Charlie's shoulders and pushed him even closer. Charlie tried to shrug him away, remembering the last time Tyler had held him by the shoulders. His mind clouded with the memory.

"I mean, really, Charlie, look at yourself," Tyler said. "Do you honestly think you're capable of doing this? Collecting the three keys, overcoming the Sovereign, and saving Lumina?" Tyler placed his elbow on top of Charlie's head.

Charlie swallowed. His stomach sank.

"You're awfully small to be a hero," Tyler said.

Charlie's mind spun, filling with every memory of torment Tyler and Michael had put him through back at the orphanage.

Tyler dropped his elbow from Charlie's head. "There's no way you can do this alone, Charlie."

Charlie lifted his eyes to stare into Tyler's face in the reflection.

"*You don't have what it takes,*" Tyler sneered.

His words stopped Charlie's heart. Instantly, he was transported back to the island cliff, where Michael had first said those words to him.

You don't have what it takes to be in the Abbott family—or any family for that matter.

Waves of emotion flooded Charlie's body. Seeing his reflection now, Charlie knew he *didn't* have what it would take—to get the key, to save Lumina, or to prove himself worthy of the guardians' bloodline.

But Tyler did.

He was tall, strong, and capable.

He'd secured his place in the Abbott family.

Perhaps he even had what it would take to be in the family of the Guardians of the Keys.

He certainly had what was needed to get the key in the amber orb.

"Look at yourself, Charlie," Tyler said, drawing Charlie's attention back to the present. "Tell me what you see when you look at yourself."

Charlie allowed his eyes to drift back to meet his own reflection in the mirror.

"What do you see?" Tyler asked again. He pushed Charlie toward the mirror. "Get closer." He nudged him again.

Charlie stood nose to nose with his own reflection.

"What do you see?" Tyler asked a third time.

Charlie's reflection stared back at him. Then, without Charlie moving, the reflection lunged at him and hissed, "Weakness!"

Charlie stumbled back from the mirror and fell to the ground.

His reflection stared back at him, still standing. Then it started to laugh.

Tyler doubled over beside the mirror, cackling. "You're afraid of your own reflection!" His words broke with laughter.

Charlie shuffled backward and scrambled to his feet.

In the mirror, his reflection pointed at him, "Weakness!" it shouted.

"Better run, Charlie," Tyler mocked. "Unless you're too weak!" he sneered.

"Weakness!" he heard his reflection shout. "Weakness!"

Without looking back, Charlie sprinted down the path. His heart pounded. His lungs burned with every labored breath.

Once outside the tree line, Charlie's eyes locked on the image of Talli and Brynn in the distance. He fixed them in his sight and raced across the dry basin floor toward them, sprinting to the sound of the voice screaming in his mind.

"Weakness, weakness, weakness …"

CHAPTER FOUR

MICHAEL SAT PROUDLY on the black stallion, shoulders back, the tail of his midnight-blue robe billowing. He was thankful for the current slower pace of travel. Cyrus, one of his father's Sovereign Guard, had been pushing the horses hard for the past two days. Though Michael was a skilled rider from growing up on the ranch, he'd never been on a horse for that long. Cyrus had barely even allowed Michael to sleep, insisting they keep moving.

But Michael wasn't tired. He hadn't been since his body buzzed with adrenaline and pulsed with the memory of the power his father had shown him.

"We're getting close to the stronghold," Cyrus called from the gray mare he rode ahead of Michael.

It was the first thing he'd said to Michael in hours. Cyrus wasn't exactly great company. But the Sovereign had insisted he was one of the best guards and the perfect guide to lead Michael to the first stronghold.

The company didn't matter to Michael, though. The journey through the city streets of Lumina had been more than enough to occupy his thoughts. Michael's mind swirled with dreams of his future.

This land was his inheritance.

He almost couldn't believe it.

As an orphan, Michael had often wondered about his parents. He certainly never imagined that he'd one day discover both he and his family were royalty from another world. Or rather, *became* royalty—all thanks to Michael's father.

His mother, on the other hand, seemed to be a different story. Michael shoved the thought away, too enraged to think about the woman who'd abandoned him and betrayed his father. He could understand why she gave up Charlie. But why Michael?

Michael shook his head, still furious at the discovery that Charlie was his twin. They looked nothing alike and had nothing in common. All the more reason he needed to protect this land from his brother. Charlie wasn't fit to rule here.

He wasn't fit for anywhere.

Which is exactly why Michael had to dispose of him.

He shifted in the saddle, unable to restrain the swell of adrenaline. In mere minutes he'd be rid of the boy he hated. In days he'd be back before his father, reaping praise and taking his seat beside the Sovereign's throne.

It was everything he never knew he wanted.

This was his kingdom. And a spectacular one at that. Michael already knew he'd love living in Lumina. He liked the darkness. He'd never been a morning person, always coming alive well past his curfew back on the ranch. Now, as the son of the Sovereign and co-ruler in this perpetual nighttime world, Michael would never have to worry about curfews or early mornings again. He smiled at the thought, then allowed his mind to drift to his first taste of glory.

It had happened during the first part of their journey, when they'd made their way through the cobblestone streets of downtown Lumina. Men and women, dressed in peasants' clothes, had seen Michael and Cyrus approach, then bowed as they passed. Michael knew they'd recognized the Sovereign's crest the horses wore on their breast collars. But he also knew, one day soon, they'd bow just because they recognized Michael's face.

But the streets of the medieval town had quickly faded from his mind as Cyrus led them northwest into the undeveloped lands of Lumina.

"We must move quickly," Cyrus had said. "There's a shorter route to the east, but it requires a difficult climb over the rugged northern mountains. We'll take the passage to the northwest. I don't know where your brother is coming from, but with these horses, we should be able to cut him off before he enters the stronghold."

Michael was confident Cyrus would be right. Michael couldn't fail. He had every advantage from his father. And Charlie had nothing.

"He has nothing and is nothing," Michael whispered to himself. He sat up straighter in the saddle and adjusted his father's bow and quiver on his shoulders. He fixed his eyes ahead on the star-studded sky. The dome of darkness protected Lumina like the shroud he'd witnessed in his father's house. The earth stretched vast beneath it, all desert now, the striking view of the snow-capped mountains long gone.

A jolt of electricity raced through Michael's body. For a moment he thought it was excitement. But then he recognized it for what it truly was.

The flow of energy returned; this time stronger. It pulsed through his body like blood.

This was the darkness. The same power he'd felt when he'd touched the shroud.

It was here. Michael knew they must be close.

Breathing deep, he focused on the sensation, knowing it was available to him to use in conquering

Charlie. His brother would have to face his darkness to succeed. All Michael had to do was give in to his.

He surrendered to the sensation, allowing his mind to fixate on only one thing—pointing an arrow at Charlie's chest.

"We're here," Cyrus said.

Michael returned his thoughts to the present and pulled his horse to a stop beside Cyrus. A vast canyon yawned in front of them. A small circular forest sat in the center. Moonlight glimmered off the tops of the trees.

"That's it," Cyrus said, pointing to the cluster. "That's the first stronghold."

"Where's Charlie?"

Cyrus shook his head. "I see no sign of him."

Michael scanned the valley. It was huge. "He could be anywhere," Michael said. He pointed to the other side of the canyon. "And he might come from any direction."

Cyrus nodded. "But he's traveling in only one direction."

Michael dismounted the horse. "Let's go then."

"You go," Cyrus said. "I can already feel the barrier. I can go no farther. You must travel the rest alone."

Michael glanced down at the stronghold, feeling the pulse grow stronger.

"Remember your mission," the guard said. "Be swift, and heed your father's warning about the stronghold's effects. Use the darkness to your benefit. Kill your brother so we can be free of his threat to Lumina."

Michael handed the reins of his horse to Cyrus.

The guard gave him a swift nod. "I shall be here waiting when you return."

Michael faced the canyon and didn't look back. He scrambled down the ravine with only the bow his father had given him and the growing swell of power in his body. It energized his steps and carried him across the valley floor to the entrance of the stronghold. He stepped across the boundary.

An electrifying buzz pulsed up his leg and through his entire body. Waves of excitement and adrenaline raced through his veins.

Michael removed the bow from his back. Every motion of his body felt fluid and effortless. Already he was harnessing the power of the darkness as his father had told him to do.

He brought his other foot across the threshold, feeling a sudden and intense disgust toward Charlie and then a delightful thrill at the thought of being rid of him.

Charlie collapsed in front of Brynn and Talli, panting. He rolled onto his back, hands clutching his heaving chest.

Brynn dropped to the ground beside him. "Charlie! Are you okay? What happened in there?"

Talli waddled to Charlie's side and scanned him head to toe with his bright-green eyes. "Are you alright, young Charlie? Did you get the key?"

Charlie shook his head. The sprint from the stronghold left him winded and unable to speak. He pointed back toward the grove of trees, now knowing that it wasn't at all the oasis it appeared to be.

"It was awful," he managed to say between gasps.

Brynn helped him into a seated position and offered him the canteen of water. "Charlie," she said in a calm voice, "you have to go back in."

"What? No way. Absolutely not. There's no way I'm going back in there."

"Charlie, you have to," Brynn said in the same quiet tone. "You're the only one who can do this."

Charlie shook his head. "What happened to you telling me I shouldn't go in there?" he asked. "Right before I went into the stronghold, *you* started having second thoughts."

"I think it was the influence of the darkness. It clouded my brain." She paused. "But Charlie, you know you have to go back in. You're Lumina's only hope." She offered him an encouraging smile. "You can do this."

Talli watched their exchange but remained silent.

"You don't get it, Brynn," Charlie said. "I *can't* do this. I tried to get the key, but I couldn't. I'm not strong enough. Besides, if I go back in there, Tyler's going to crush me."

"Tyler?" Brynn asked.

"Ahhh …" Talli finally spoke up. "This must be the darkness the Sage said you'll have to overcome."

Charlie turned to face the Roush. "You don't understand, Talli. Tyler is one of the kids from the orphanage. He's Michael's best friend. And the last time I saw him, he was ready to help Michael bury me in the ground. Not to mention, that place is horrifying." Charlie stared at the stronghold and shook off a shiver, remembering the terrifying reflection of himself. In a low voice he said, "There's no way I'm going back in there."

Talli draped a white wing over his shoulder. "Charlie, you *can* do this. Remember what the Sage said: everything you need to overcome the stronghold is already inside you."

Charlie shook his head. "I don't even understand what that means. Besides, I have nothing inside me. That's the problem. I don't have what it takes."

"Oh, but you do." The Roush's eyes twinkled. "Soon you will see it," Talli said, "*and* understand it."

Charlie drew a deep breath. He cast a glance at Brynn.

"I believe in you, Charlie," she said.

He bit his lip, hesitating.

"If you don't go back in," she said, "we might as well return to the Sage. Then we can each return home."

Charlie glanced back at the stronghold, reminding himself once again that he had no home.

He exhaled loudly, rose to his feet, then dusted off his pants. Without another word, he left Brynn and Talli and trudged toward the stronghold, dreading it with every step.

The distance stretched in front of him like an eternal barren valley, but it took mere seconds to cross. Charlie hesitated at the tree line, feeling the thrumming pulse of darkness surge through his body. Dread rose within him even stronger than the first time he'd entered. He fixed his mind on Brynn's words.

She believed in him.

And if Charlie *didn't* do this, he'd have to return to a place that was not home. The only way out, it seemed, was through the stronghold.

Charlie stepped forward, feeling the ground under his boots shift from solid earth to soft soil. The next thing he knew, the trees enveloped him, drawing him into the dark forest as if by force and not by his own will.

The fog was denser this time. As were the trees. Snakelike vines draped from the branches and threatened to ensnare him. The Spanish moss was so thick now, it blocked portions of his view. Even the darkness seemed heavier.

He continued down the path, fixing his eyes on the gazebo he knew was there but couldn't see.

"I just need to get the key and get out of here," Charlie said to himself.

As the words left his lips, the first sign of the gazebo came into view. Charlie lengthened his stride then quickened his pace.

"Get the key," he chanted to himself. "Get the key and get out. Get the key and get—"

Charlie skidded to a stop.

The trees that lined the path closed in around him.

The trail narrowed.

He blinked, thinking his eyes must be playing tricks on him. But they weren't.

The forest moved, shrinking the path that led to the gazebo.

The stronghold was changing.

Charlie took off in a sprint toward the key, but the trees pressed in tighter on both sides. He pushed his legs to move faster but was forced to turn right off the trail when a giant oak tree erupted from the ground, blocking his path entirely.

He darted through the underbrush, leaping over gnarled roots and dodging thick dangling vines. He tried to dive between the trunks of two trees, but they snapped together, forming a wall. Charlie slid to a stop, then maneuvered left. He made it only a few feet before a curtain of impenetrable vines dropped from the branches.

He turned back the way he came, seeing the main trail in the distance, its path now clear. Rocks sprang up from the earth, making the trek difficult, but finally, Charlie's feet hit the clear path.

Again, he took off in the direction of the gazebo and the key. But this time, the trees slid together, tree against tree, sealing Charlie out of the clearing.

He turned around to find another way, then froze.

A door stood on the path.

Charlie backed away from it. "No," he said. "No, no, no."

He heard a loud groan behind him and turned to see the branches of a tree reaching for him, pushing him toward the door.

"No!" Charlie shouted.

But he had no choice. He had to move.

Thick vines lashed out at him like whips, forcing him closer and closer to the door. Charlie spun to scan the forest and take in his options.

Trees closed in all around him. The only way to

avoid the door was to dart around and take the path behind it.

He raced toward it, willing his legs to get him there before the door became his only option.

Five feet from the door, the trees cut him off.

"No!" Charlie shouted.

The massive oaks pressed in on all sides.

Terror flooded Charlie's body. He inched toward the door, imagining that Tyler would burst through at any moment.

The forest narrowed even more, forcing Charlie's back against the door.

The scent of the woods was suffocating, the darkness thicker than night. The wood panel dug into his back.

A branch from the nearest tree reached out like a gnarled hand. It grasped at Charlie's face. A vine slithered up his leg.

Charlie reached behind him. His trembling hand wrapped around the cold metal of the handle. Despite the voice in his head that told him not to, Charlie twisted the knob and fell backward through the door.

On his back, Charlie stared up at a clear starry sky. Cool evening air wrapped around his body. He sat up. The door stood open before him, but the trees and vines were gone. Now he could see straight through the door, and the image on the other side was a continuation of the scene on this side.

Charlie stood. A familiar field stretched before him on either side of the door. He turned to the left, seeing the mansionlike ranch of Saint Francis's Boys and Girls Home a short distance away. Spotlights illuminated the giant white farmhouse. Charlie heard laughter behind him. Firelight from a flickering bonfire caught his eye. He started toward it, hesitated, turned, then closed the door.

The sound of laughter and voices grew louder as Charlie approached. He was a few feet away when the light of the bonfire illuminated the familiar faces of the people who sat around it. It was the children from the orphanage. No one noticed him. He searched the circle for Sarah. When he saw her, he moved closer.

"Sarah?" he said.

He noted the hesitation in his voice, wondering if Sarah heard it too. Wondering if she could hear his unspoken apology for the way he'd treated her back on the island. Wondering if she'd forgive him for their fight.

"Sarah?"

Her eyes stared through him. All the kids did. It was like he wasn't even there.

"Kurtis," Charlie said, waving a hand in front of the boy's face. But again, it was like he couldn't see Charlie.

"He doesn't belong here," someone said.

Charlie turned to see Michael lean toward the fire

and poke it with a stick. He looked up into the faces of the other children. "We have to get rid of Charlie," he said.

Charlie froze. He started to speak but was cut off by Tyler.

"Yeah," Tyler said, "Michael's right. Charlie doesn't belong here. There's no way we can allow him to get adopted."

The other children around the fire nodded.

"Exactly," Michael said. "He adds nothing of value to this family. He's no Abbott."

"That's not true!" Charlie shouted. "Sarah, tell them that's not true!"

But Sarah said nothing. And still no one acknowledged his presence.

"Agreed," Milo chimed in. "He's not smart like Kurtis or awesome like me."

Raegan rolled her eyes but said, "Milo's right. There's nothing special about Charlie. Everyone else in our family is special. He doesn't fit in."

Even Maxine nodded in agreement.

Charlie stepped into the ring of firelight. He rushed over to Sarah and tapped her arm, but she didn't feel him. "Sarah!" He shouted and shook her shoulders. She moved under the weight of his hands, but still she looked straight through him.

"Guys, please listen to me," Charlie said. "I can be

better. I promise I have something to offer. Just give me another chance!"

"I can't believe Mr. Abbott even brought him here," Michael said. "What was he thinking?"

"He probably didn't realize what a dud Charlie would end up being," Tyler said.

Michael nodded. "He'll kick him out before his twelve-month probationary period is even up. I mean, why would he waste his time with someone as useless as him?"

"Don't say that!" Charlie shouted. "I'm not useless. *I'm not useless!*"

He knelt before Sarah and tried to angle his face directly in her line of sight. Her eyes were fixed on Michael, but she said nothing.

"What do you think, Sarah?" Michael asked.

Charlie stood and slowly turned to look at the boy he now knew to be his twin brother.

"I mean, you've spent the most time with him," Michael said. "We all agree Charlie needs to go. What's your vote?"

Sarah straightened her shoulders. Her face betrayed nothing.

"Well?" Michael asked.

Sarah cleared her throat. "His parents abandoned him," she said.

Charlie stiffened.

Sarah's lips ticked to the side. "I think it's obvious why. He's useless."

Charlie crumpled to the ground. "No! That's not true!"

But in his head, Charlie could hear his own voice confirming every word they said.

No matter how hard I try, I'll never have anything to offer.

Charlie's hands clutched the sides of his head. "Sarah, please! I'm sorry! I'm so sorry! Please don't listen to them. Please give me a second chance. Tell them I'm worth a second chance."

But in his heart, Charlie knew he wasn't.

"So we get rid of him then?" Michael said.

Tyler nodded.

Milo raised a fist in the air. "Yes! Shut him out!" he shouted.

In his mind, Charlie heard the echo of his own voice saying, *Your existence is a burden. You never should've been born.*

Everyone except Sarah joined in the chant, "Shut him out! Shut him out!"

Charlie took a step back. "No," he murmured.

"Shut him out! Shut him out!"

Charlie backed farther away. He scanned the faces of the other kids. Everyone stared at Michael, who fueled their hatred.

"Sarah?" Michael asked. "We all need to agree. What do you think we should do?"

Charlie's eyes locked on Sarah's face. For the first time, her gaze seemed to drift to his. "Shut him out," she said.

"No!" Charlie screamed, his voice raw with emotion.

Sarah's eyes locked on Charlie's. She stood. The sound of the other kids' voices slowly faded. Then they all turned their gaze to him. Their chanting ceased.

Sarah took a step toward Charlie, and this time he knew she saw him.

She tilted her head to the side. "Don't pretend like you don't know how worthless you are, Charlie."

Charlie stumbled backward. He tripped as he turned.

Laughter rose from the group like the sparks from the bonfire. Charlie sprinted across the field of Mr. Abbott's ranch, wishing with every heart-pounding step that he'd never come, never met Mr. Abbott or any of the kids, and most of all wishing he'd never been born.

Charlie could hear the kids behind him, hear their evil cackles and chanting words. "Shut him out! Shut him out!"

The sound of their chant synced with the pound of his feet and beat of his heart. They were behind him. Chasing him. Hunting him.

With tears streaming down his cheeks, Charlie raced across the last few yards of the field, never looking back. He had to get out of here. He didn't belong and never would. With a gut-wrenching sob, Charlie wrapped his fingers around the doorknob and pulled, then plunged through the door.

CHAPTER FIVE

CHARLIE FELL THROUGH the door and onto his knees, eyes clenched shut, tears streaking his cheeks. His chest heaved as he gulped air. The chanting was gone now, as was the bonfire scene and ranch.

It hadn't been real.

Just like everything else in this stronghold, it was an illusion. But the emotions it stirred up were anything but fake.

He'd never felt so raw. Of all the times he'd been bullied, this experience was the worst.

Charlie leaned forward, gripping the earth with his fingers. He pressed his head against the cool soil, curling into himself.

As an orphan, Charlie had felt trapped before. He'd been stuck in a number of bad foster situations over the years and had to put up with countless bullies. Those trials had trained him to withstand Michael's horrible behavior. But perseverance failed him now. He felt trapped in a new way. And now, more than anything, Charlie wanted to give up.

He sighed against the ground, knowing that even if he did give up and leave the stronghold, he had nowhere good to go.

"Maybe I can just stay right here," he muttered, eyes closed, body curled up against the ground. Perhaps if he didn't move from this place, no other terrible things could happen to him.

But even as he considered the thought, he knew it wasn't possible.

He was in a stronghold, after all. If Charlie had learned anything, it was that *all* of the terrible things could happen to him here. And all at once it seemed.

Charlie drew in a deep breath. The scent of the damp earth filled his nostrils. Mustering up his last molecule of strength, Charlie opened his eyes.

There, at the center of the clearing, the gazebo stood in silence, mocking him.

Charlie pushed up from the ground, reminding himself that the only way out was through. He had to find a way to get the key.

"Maybe it's just about surviving," Charlie said, eyes fixed on the amber orb and the sapphire key inside.

The Sage had said it was about overcoming the darkness.

"Well, I'm still here," Charlie said to himself. "Maybe I've already overcome it."

Charlie grabbed a fist-sized stone from the ground, crossed to the gazebo, and ascended the steps. He placed one hand on the amber orb, feeling its subtle pulse of power. He stared at it for a long time, willing the resin to crack, mentally pleading with the key to emerge from its prison. But nothing happened.

A wave of frustration surged through Charlie's body. He reared his hand back and screamed, then slammed the stone against the orb.

Once, twice, three times he cracked the rock against the amber. On the fourth time, he missed, accidently smashing his knuckles against the orb instead.

Overwhelmed and in pain, Charlie screamed again. Without looking, he spun and hurled the rock into the forest. But instead of landing with a thud on the ground, the stone filled the clearing with a loud shatter—the sound of breaking glass.

Charlie looked up.

"No," he uttered. "No, no, no."

Another wooden door stood between two trees, this one with a shattered mirror hanging on its paneled surface.

Charlie trembled. "No."

He had to get out!

He spun. Another door appeared on the other side of the clearing, this one's mirror intact.

He leaped down the steps, sprinted to the trees, and veered to the right, desperate to get out of the clearing. But the moment he turned, another door appeared between two trees, blocking his path. He tried to dash around it, but again, another door.

Charlie's feet faltered. He stumbled back. He heard a woosh behind him and turned to see door after door materialize between the trees that encircled the clearing. Each one fitted with a mirror.

He scanned the area, searching for an opening. When he found one, he sprinted toward it with everything he had.

His mind screamed at him to forget the key. He had to get out of here.

But as soon as Charlie reached the opening, another mirrored door appeared.

Charlie skidded to a stop and immediately changed course. He ran the perimeter of the clearing, but doors appeared faster than his feet could move. Everywhere he turned he saw door, tree, door, tree.

He froze and scanned the forest. There was nowhere left to run.

A familiar voice spoke behind him. "You've really done it now."

Charlie spun to see his reflection in one of the mirrors.

It spoke to him.

"Classic Charlie," the reflection said. "You're a failure every time."

"Yeah," another reflection said. "*F* is for *failure*." It doubled over in a fit of laughter.

Fear flooded Charlie's body. The sound of laughter multiplied as all the reflections came to life, each one jeering and taunting.

"You're a failure, Charlie!"

"If only you had been stronger!"

"If only you had been smarter!"

"If only you hadn't been so useless!"

Charlie backed away from the reflections, but there was no escaping the sound of his own voice.

"Admit it, Charlie. Even *you* hate yourself."

Under his breath, Charlie said, "I do hate myself." His voice cracked. "I *hate* being me. That's why I'm envious of everyone else."

Once again, the reflections burst into fits of laughter.

Charlie slowly turned in a circle, taking in his reflection in each mirror, each one spewing hateful words at him.

He tried to look away, but there was no escaping himself.

Defeated, Charlie moved to take a seat on the gazebo stairs, but one of the reflections across the clearing caught his eye. This one didn't laugh. It didn't speak. Its eyes weren't filled with hatred.

It held up a hand and motioned Charlie to come.

He hesitated, then walked across the clearing, trying to shut out the sound of his own voice.

He stopped in front of the mirror.

A subtle smiled curled on his reflection's lips. "What do you see, Charlie?" it asked.

Charlie paused, remembering what had happened the last time he was asked this question.

"Weakness," Charlie said.

The golden-brown eyes of his reflection stared at him. "I don't see weakness," the image said. "I see a boy brave enough to enter a stronghold and face his own darkness." The reflection paused, then asked again, "What do you see, Charlie?"

Charlie sighed but this time stopped to take in his own appearance. He was wearing the tunic and pants the Sage had given him. The clothes were too big for his small frame. He *did* look weak, but Charlie tried to see beyond that.

His eyes scanned his reflection from head to toe, but all Charlie saw was a boy who looked dirty, exhausted, and spent of any strength he may have once had.

Charlie cleared his throat, then spoke. His voice

sounded even weaker than he appeared. "I see a nothing and a nobody," he said to his own reflection. "There's nothing special about me."

The reflection in the mirror tilted its head to the side. A smile flickered in the corner of its lips. "That's not what I see," it said. "I see something very special— you." The reflection paused. The chant of the voices from the other mirrors faded. The reflection in front of him somehow became brighter, clearer. It straightened its shoulders and lifted its head. It moved independently of Charlie, not appearing at all like it belonged to someone such as him. And for a moment, Charlie felt envious of the confident-looking boy in the mirror, the boy who looked just like him—and also like someone else entirely. The reflection's smile spread across his face as if he knew what Charlie was thinking. Then it leaned in. "You *are* special, Charlie," it said. "What makes you so special is the fact that you don't need to be special."

The words pierced Charlie's heart. They came from the lips of his own reflection, but as they landed in his ears, he heard them as if they were spoken by someone else. And hadn't they been?

An image of Sarah filled Charlie's mind, and he was back in the library at the ranch, seated in the window seat across from her.

"You *are* special, Charlie," she'd said to him. "What

makes you so special is the fact that you don't need to be special."

It felt like a lifetime ago that Sarah had spoken those words. They'd felt more like an insult than a compliment. Now he heard them differently.

"What makes me special is the fact that I don't need to be special," he whispered to himself. Uncertainty lingered in his voice. But as he spoke aloud, words from another friend—a new friend—came rushing back to him.

In his mind, Charlie saw Talli sitting on the head of the horse, green eyes wide with excitement and wonder. He heard Talli's voice as if the Roush stood right beside him.

Instead of changing into someone different, you could choose to become the person you've always been but didn't realize you were.

Again, Charlie's reflection smiled as if reading Charlie's thoughts.

And couldn't it, though? Wasn't this a reflection of himself?

Charlie turned and scanned the countless other mirrors. The taunting had ceased. The other reflections were silent now, watching, waiting.

Charlie faced the mirror with the reflection who spoke kindly.

"What do you see, Charlie?" it asked a third time.

The smile lingered on its lips as it waited for Charlie's response.

Charlie stared into his own eyes, then said, "I see me."

This time, the lips of his reflection matched his word for word.

"I see a boy who has bullied himself more than any other child possibly could." He paused. "I *am* special," he said to himself. "I'm special because I'm Charlie. I'm special because I don't need to be the strongest or the bravest or the smartest. I'm special because I'm me. I don't need to become someone else, because the person I am is already pretty great. I just didn't realize it." This time, Charlie felt the smile on his face as he saw it in the reflection. "I don't want to be like anyone else," he said. "I just want to be me."

A piercing white beam of light sprang from the mirror. Charlie jumped back. His reflection pointed to something behind him. Charlie turned to see the beam of light reflect off every other mirror in the clearing. Each of his reflections wore a smile. Charlie glanced down, seeing the same brilliant light pour from his own hand. He lifted it to his face. It was beautiful. A warm feeling flooded Charlie's body, and an intense pulsing sensation formed in his hand. It reminded him of the sensation from the amber orb.

Charlie's eyes found the gazebo. The orb hovered

in the same place, but now it hummed with energy. Charlie took one final look at his reflections, then ran to the gazebo and climbed the steps to stand before the key.

Light continued to pour from his hand. Charlie held it over the amber orb, feeling the pulse in his hand sync with the vibration in the golden resin that held the key. The light from his hand pierced the orb, which acted like a prism and cast its light throughout the entire stronghold. And for a moment, Charlie's surroundings appeared as bright as the light of day.

Words formed deep inside Charlie, then slipped from his lips. "The light of self-love overcomes the darkness of self-hatred. This is what it means to overcome envy."

Around him, the mirrored doors vanished, leaving Charlie alone with the key.

He hesitated, then placed his hand on the surface of the amber orb. It dissolved beneath his fingers, and the key clinked onto the pedestal.

Michael crept through the forest like a hunter stalking his prey, feeling every step magnify the intensity of his own darkness.

"Where are you, Charlie?" he said under his breath.

Michael's fingers wrapped tighter around the bow. His eyes scanned the darkness for the brother he'd soon be rid of.

A sound like a whooshing gust of wind roared to life behind Michael. He turned to see a mirror mounted to a wooden door. He stepped closer, expecting to see a powerful image of himself, dressed in his royal robe. Instead, a different reflection greeted him.

It was Charlie.

But more surprising than seeing his twin show up as his reflection in a mirror was the emotion it sparked within Michael.

A deep sense of envy flooded Michael's body—envy of Charlie.

Michael backed away, confused, and not understanding where the thoughts and feelings had come from.

Then he remembered Cyrus's warning.

"Remember your mission," the guard had said. "Be swift, and heed your father's warning about the stronghold's effects. Use the darkness to your benefit. Kill your brother so we can be free of his threat to Lumina."

Michael approached the mirror until he was only a breath away. He stared into the golden-brown eyes of his brother—into the image of everything he hated. He lingered, allowing the hatred to fuel him.

Chaos erupted behind Michael.

He spun and scanned the area. Light pierced the darkness on the trail. The forest exploded with a thrum of energy.

Something was happening.

Michael sprinted toward it.

The trail ended between two trees. Michael slowed when he reached them. A circular clearing opened just beyond the trees, and a gazebo sat in the middle.

And in the center of it all was Charlie. He ascended the stairs. Light poured from the palm of his right hand.

Michael darted behind one the trees but peered around the side to watch.

A pedestal sat in the center of the gazebo, and an amber-colored orb hovered above it.

The sphere reminded Michael of the shrouded orb his father had shown him in the House of Lumina—the orb that was his power, *his inheritance.*

Another wave of envy flashed through Michael's body. He wouldn't let Charlie steal what belonged to *him.*

Michael drew an arrow from his quiver, allowing his own darkness to surge.

He watched as Charlie placed his hand above the orb, then pressed his palm to its surface. The amber dissolved beneath his fingers and released something. It clinked against the pedestal.

Michael could only assume it was the key.

Furious, he stepped out from behind the tree, nocked an arrow, and drew his bow. He set Charlie in his sights, then stepped closer.

A twig snapped beneath his foot.

Charlie spun, his hand hovering over the key.

And for a second, they locked eyes.

Again, Michael felt the wave of envy flood his body, and he hated it. The sensation fueled him.

He narrowed his eyes. "Bye-bye, brother," Michael said under his breath, then loosed the arrow.

Charlie's palm slammed down on top of the key.

Then his body vanished.

The arrow sailed through the gazebo, right through the spot where Charlie had stood, then flew out the other side. It sank into the trunk of one of the trees.

Michael ran up the steps of the gazebo.

Both Charlie and the key were gone.

Michael's hatred flared into a fiery rage, now accompanied by an intense dread of having to face his father.

For the first time in his life, Michael had failed.

And he'd failed because of Charlie.

He slung the bow over his shoulder and stormed down the stairs toward the trail that would take him back to Cyrus.

He hoped to see Charlie on his way out, because

Michael knew the next time he saw his brother, he wouldn't miss.

Charlie blinked, then took in his surroundings. He stood in the center of the dark desert canyon directly outside the stronghold. He could see Brynn and Talli in the distance.

A warm sensation pulsed in his right hand. Charlie slowly uncurled his fingers to reveal the key. The diamond-shaped sapphire glittered in the moonlight.

"I did it," Charlie whispered to himself.

He squeezed his fingers tightly around the key, allowing its warm vibration to fill his hand and fuel his body. He cast a quick glance at the stronghold, then placed the key in the leather pouch he wore around his waist.

The Sage was right. The Sovereign *had* sent Michael.

And not just to stop Charlie.

He'd sent Michael to kill him.

Charlie allowed the thought to sink in.

It was one thing to process that Michael had nearly killed him. It was another altogether to realize Charlie's own father wanted him dead.

Charlie scanned the entrance to the stronghold. He didn't see Michael, but that didn't mean he wasn't in pursuit. If Charlie knew Michael like he thought he did, then Michael wouldn't delay in hunting Charlie down. Especially now that Charlie had the first key.

The first key.

He lingered on the thought for only a second, then took off toward Brynn and Talli. The distance across the desert basin seemed much shorter this time.

Expressions of relief marked Brynn's and Talli's faces when Charlie finally reached them. He breathed heavily but managed to get the words out.

"I got it," he panted. "I've got the first key."

Brynn's face lit up. She ran to Charlie and wrapped him in a hug. "I knew you could do it."

Charlie stepped out of her arms, caught off guard. "Thanks," he said.

Talli waddled toward him. "Well done, young Charlie. I knew you could do it even more than she did." The Roush winked at Brynn.

She rolled her eyes, and Charlie wondered what the two of them had been chatting about while he was inside the stronghold.

"You were right," Charlie said to Talli.

"Of course I was right," Talli said. "But about what particularly?"

Charlie fought back a smile. "Everything I needed was already inside me."

"Oh yes, that, well … I'm happy to have helped."

Talli bowed. "Now, you must tell us everything about your adventure."

Charlie cast a glance over his shoulder at the dark forest. The sense of accomplishment he'd felt was quickly overwhelmed by a feeling of dread. "I will," he said. "But not now. Michael's in there, but he won't be for long."

"Yeah," Brynn said. "We need to leave now if we're going to make it to the second stronghold before your brother. Our journey will take four days from here. We'll have to travel fast."

CHAPTER SIX

SARAH SAT ON THE BEACH, staring out at the murky ocean depths. Waves crashed against the shore and drowned out the sound of the other kids. They were several yards down the beach, setting up camp under the rocky overhang.

By the time Sarah had returned with Maxine and Kurtis, Becca and Joey had created eight stacks of palm fronds to use as sleeping mats, since they no longer had the tarps to keep them out of the sand. Now the two of them gathered scraps of dry wood for a fire while Maxine and Kurtis removed the edible meat from the Malabar chestnuts.

Tyler, Milo, and Raegan weren't back yet, and there was still no sign of Charlie or Michael.

Sarah wiggled her bare toes in the sand, then reached into her pocket to pull out the water bottle with the strange cocoon. The sun was starting to set, and the dim light gave the caterpillar even more of a glowing appearance.

Voices approached. Sarah shoved the bottle back into her pocket, jumped to her feet, and dusted the sand from her skort.

Halfway between their camp and where she stood, Milo stumbled onto the beach from the wooded tree line. He wavered on his feet, glanced down the beach in her direction, then headed toward the rocky overhang. The T-shirt he wore like a sling appeared full. Sarah wondered what he'd found.

Tyler and Raegan stumbled out of the trees behind Milo and followed him. Raegan carried her hoodie, also stuffed full, and Tyler trailed one step behind her, swaying as they made their way toward the camp. The sound of their laughter drifted above the crash of the waves and beckoned Sarah with the promise of good news. She jogged down the beach toward them. Maybe they'd discovered their missing supplies? Or better yet, a sign of Charlie or Michael? Sarah quickened her pace and caught up with them as they joined the rest of their group.

"Look what we found!" Raegan held up her hoodie, but the way she had it tied, no one could see what was inside.

"Did you find our stuff?" Maxine asked.

Tyler was still chuckling about something when he turned to Maxine. "What stuff?"

Sarah stepped closer. "Our stuff that you insisted was stolen," Sarah said. She stood directly across from Tyler. The rest of the kids had circled around them.

"Oh, that," Tyler said. He shrugged. "Nah, we didn't find it." His eyes were wide, his pupils larger than normal. "But we found something better. Show 'em what we found, Milo!" His voice was odd, his words slurred.

"Tada!" Milo made a big showy display of removing his T-shirt sling and dumped a pile of waxy, purple fruit onto the sand. Raegan emptied her hoodie onto the pile as well, revealing even more of the oblong, baseball-sized fruit.

"What is it?" Maxine asked.

"Only the best thing you'll ever eat." Milo said. "It tastes like cotton candy!"

"No," Raegan said. "Strawberry shortcake."

"Mixed with cherry cordial ice cream," Tyler said, doubling over with laughter. The three of them dissolved into giggles.

Kurtis picked up the fruit. "I've never seen this fruit before."

"Me either," Becca said.

Sarah nudged one with her foot. The fruit looked

like a cross between a plum and an eggplant.

Kurtis pulled the fruit apart. "Weird," he said. "You guys ate this?" He looked to Milo.

"Ate it? We devoured it!" Milo said.

Sarah noted the light-purple flesh and the bright-red pit in the center. The smell reached her. It was sickly sweet.

"Yeah, I've definitely never seen this before," Kurtis said. "You shouldn't eat any more of it. It could be poisonous."

"Poison shmoison." Milo slapped his thigh. "If poison tastes this delicious, then—" He didn't finish his sentence, overcome with another fit of laughter.

"You guys are acting funny," Maxine said.

Milo paused his giggles long enough to look at her and say, "I'm always funny."

"No, she's right," Becca said. "You guys are acting weird. It's like you're intoxicated or something."

"We're fine," Tyler insisted. "Here, Squirt," he said to Maxine. Tyler stooped to pick up a piece of fruit, then handed it to her. "Try one. You'll love it." He ruffled the top of her head.

Sarah shifted on her feet, watching the way Maxine's eyes lit up the way they always did when Tyler acted brotherly toward her.

Maxine sniffed the fruit.

Sarah placed herself between Tyler and Maxine,

then took the fruit from the girl's hand. "Don't eat that."

Tyler's hand fell heavy on Sarah's shoulder. He spun her around. His laughter was gone. The strange look in his eyes remained, but now it was magnified by a wild rage.

"What are you doing?" Tyler demanded.

"Maxine doesn't need to eat that," Sarah said calmly. "We don't know what kind of fruit it is, and clearly it's having an effect on you guys. She shouldn't eat it. None of us should. Kurtis is right. It could be poisonous."

Tyler jabbed Sarah in the shoulder with his finger. "The only poison on this island is you."

Sarah narrowed her eyes. "What are you talking about?"

Tyler's voice was low. "You know what I'm talking about." His lips twitched. "*Murderer.*"

A wave of heat flooded Sarah's body. A lightheaded feeling flooded her brain.

"That's right," he said, not giving her a chance to respond. "You're a murderer."

Sarah straightened her shoulders. "What are you even talking about, Tyler?"

"Oh, I think you know. You helped kill Michael."

Sarah shook her head. "Are you nuts? Where are you coming up with this? Why do you keep insisting that Michael is dead?"

"Because he is!" Tyler shouted. "Where else could he

be? And we found his blood! Admit it, Sarah, Charlie killed Michael. You know it! You know where his body is, and you know where Charlie is hiding!" He lowered his face to hers. "And you helped kill him."

"You're insane." Sarah turned to storm away, but Tyler spun her around again.

"Don't you dare walk away from me!"

"Get your hands off me!" Sarah said.

"Or what?" Tyler shoved her.

Something inside Sarah snapped. She shoved him back.

A dark look crossed Tyler's face. When he pushed her this time, the full brunt of his weight barreled into Sarah. She fell backward into the sand.

"Get her!" Tyler shouted.

The next few seconds unfolded in a blur.

Milo and Raegan tackled Sarah. Raegan grabbed her arms and held them tight while Milo pinned her legs. A crazed laughter bubbled from Tyler's lips.

"What are you doing?" Sarah shouted. "Let me go!"

"Let her go!" Becca screamed.

Maxine's sobs reached Sarah's ears.

Sarah kicked her legs, but Milo held firm.

"Stop! Get off me! Milo, why are you doing this?"

"Because Tyler's right," Milo said. A wild look crossed his mud-painted face. "You did it. You killed Michael. I know you did because the island told me!"

"It spoke to you too?" Tyler asked.

Milo nodded.

"Stop!" Maxine wailed. "Tyler, please make them stop!"

Raegan's laughter sounded just as crazed as Tyler's.

Sarah continued her struggle, but she was no match for both Milo and Raegan.

Tyler knelt beside Sarah. He pulled a pocketknife from his waistband.

"Tell us where you're hiding Charlie," he said with a sneer.

Sarah tugged her arms against Raegan's grip. "I don't know where he is!"

Tyler flicked open the knife. "See this," he said, examining the blade in front of her face. "Michael had the same one. We bought them together on our trip to Florida." He glanced down at his blue Hawaiian-print shirt. "The same time we bought these shirts. Do you know why we have matching pocketknives and shirts?" he asked.

"Tyler, stop!" Becca shouted. "You're going to hurt someone."

"Leave Sarah alone!" Maxine wailed.

Sarah, filled with rage and fear, pierced Tyler with her stare but said nothing.

"Because Michael and I are best friends, brothers even, according to Mr. Abbott." Tyler lowered the knife toward Sarah's face. She leaned away from the blade. "You can tell me what happened to Michael on your own," he said. "Or I can make you tell me."

Maxine dropped to the sand and wedged herself between Tyler and Sarah. She slammed an open palm against Tyler's chest. "Stop!" she screamed. Tyler quickly drew the knife away from the younger girl. "What's wrong with you?" Maxine demanded. Tears stained her cheeks.

A brief moment of clarity registered on Tyler's face, then disappeared. He burst into laughter.

Raegan released Sarah's arms and rolled to her back, giggling hysterically.

"Get off me!" Sarah said to Milo. This time he released her legs. He, too, fell into a fit of laughter.

Tyler stood and sauntered over to the pile of fruit, picked one up and took a giant bite. Juice dripped down his chin.

Sarah stood on shaking legs. Her hands trembled.

"Maxine's right," Becca said. "What in the world is wrong with you, Tyler?"

"You could have really hurt me," Sarah said to Tyler. Her voice trembled with the adrenaline that coursed through her body. She rubbed her wrists. They felt bruised from Raegan's grip.

He took another juicy bite of the fruit then said, "It was just a joke."

But Sarah had seen the look in Tyler's eyes when he'd pointed the knife at her. This was no joke. More than ever, Tyler believed that Sarah and Charlie had done something to hurt Michael.

Kurtis stepped forward, wringing his hands. He looked at Tyler nervously then said, "I think this fruit might have psychoactive properties."

"What does that mean?" Sarah asked.

"It's messing with their minds," Kurtis explained. "It's having a chemical effect on them."

"Agreed," Becca said. She stomped over to the pile of fruit and started shoving it back inside Raegan's hoodie and Milo's T-shirt.

"Hey!" Tyler shouted. "What are you doing?"

"Kurtis is right," Becca said. "This fruit is messing with your head."

"That's ridiculous," Tyler said. "It's just fruit. And there's plenty more where that came from."

Becca stopped to stare at him. "Where?"

"On the other side of the island," Milo said. "There's tons of it."

Becca hoisted the two shirts full of purple fruit and marched toward the water.

"What are you doing with that?" Tyler ran after her.

The rest of the group followed. Sarah trailed in the back, still stunned by the attack.

"I'm getting rid of this," Becca said and tossed the

whole load of fruit into the ocean. When she finished, she returned the shirts to Milo and Raegan. "No purple fruit," she said. "No going to the other side of the island. Got it?"

"You can't tell us what to do," Tyler said through gritted teeth.

"Look," Becca said. "Someone needs to be in charge here. Someone level-headed, and that's clearly not the three of you." She pointed at Tyler, Milo, and Raegan. "If we're going to get off this island, we have to stick together, and we certainly can't be threatening one another with knives. Understood?"

Tyler just stared at her.

"Give me your knife." Becca held out her hand.

Tyler didn't move.

"Give it to me," she said again.

Tyler rolled his eyes, then handed over the knife.

"Are we all in agreement?" Becca asked. "No purple fruit."

"Agreed," Kurtis said.

Joey nodded.

"I agree," Maxine said.

"Tyler?" Becca fixed him with a stare.

Sarah saw his jaw clench. "Agreed," he muttered.

"Milo? Raegan?"

"Fine," Raegan said.

Milo started to protest. "But what about what the island said—"

Tyler elbowed him in the ribs.

Milo kicked at the sand and huffed. "Fine. I agree."

"Good," Becca said. She brushed her hands together then marched back toward their camp. Joey, Kurtis, and Maxine followed.

Sarah was left standing near the water's edge with Tyler, Milo, and Raegan. They didn't speak a word to her, all three of them staring out at the spot where Becca had thrown the food.

Sarah could tell by the look on Tyler's face that this wouldn't be the last of the purple fruit for him.

He caught her staring.

Still shaken, Sarah turned to walk back toward the camp with the others. As she neared the overhang, she cast one last look at Tyler, realizing, now more than ever, she needed to find Charlie and Michael. Because until she did, Sarah would be wearing a target on her back, and Tyler was the one holding the arrow.

The next morning, Sarah woke to the sound of Joey shouting.

"Wake up, wake up!" he said. "Guys, you've gotta come see this."

Sarah bolted upright, and Maxine stirred beside her. The rest of the kids rushed from the camp toward the surf where Joey stood, pointing at the horizon.

"C'mon," Sarah said to Maxine. "Let's go see what's happening."

They reached the group, and Sarah wiped her sleepy eyes. She rubbed them again when she saw what had caught everyone's attention.

On the horizon, where there had once only been open ocean, sat a landmass.

Maxine gasped. "Sarah, what's that?"

Shaking her head in disbelief, Sarah lightly touched her pocket where she kept the water bottle with the cocoon. "Another island," she said.

CHAPTER SEVEN

MICHAEL STOOD in the Sovereign's throne room, head held high despite failing to destroy Charlie. On the two-day journey back to the House of Lumina, he could think of nothing but his shame. Cyrus had been quiet during their travels, magnifying Michael's disappointment in himself and fanning the flame of his hatred.

"You failed," the Sovereign said from his throne. His voice boomed through the chamber. "Charles has a key. Do you realize what's at stake?"

Michael stared past his father, unable to look into those cloudy gray eyes of judgment. "Forgive me, Father. It won't happen again."

"Of that I'm certain," the Sovereign said in a low tone. The Chancellor stood beside him.

Michael swallowed hard, feeling the weight of his father's disappointment. He forced himself to stand tall.

"It seems your brother is a more challenging opponent than you led me to believe," the Sovereign said. Michael started to protest, but the Sovereign cut him off. "We don't have time for your excuses, boy. Charles is no doubt on his way to the second stronghold. We must act now."

Michael shifted from foot to foot. "I fired the arrow as you told me to do," he said. "But Charlie vanished, and the arrow missed."

"No," the Sovereign said in an icy tone. "The arrow didn't miss. You did."

Michael didn't dare argue.

"Charles would've been transported directly outside the stronghold once he obtained the key. He bested you." The Sovereign paused dramatically, his harsh words echoing through the chamber. "If, as you said, you left right away, then Charles can't be far ahead of you. There are only two routes to the second stronghold: the way you came through the mountain passage, or the more northern route. Either way, he'll have to traverse the highlands. And this time of year, they're covered in snow. Fortunately, you have the benefit of my resources. Charles does not."

"Then I'll leave now," Michael said, pushing his shoulders back and his chin up. "I'll make up for the lost time and cut him off before he arrives."

"You will do no such thing," the Sovereign said. "Did you even look at the map I gave you?"

This time, Michael lowered his eyes. His insides boiled with rage at his own stupidity. "No, sir."

"I thought so," the Sovereign said. "You already gave Charles a head start. It's not possible for you to get ahead of him now."

The Sovereign's words cut deeper than Michael thought they could.

"You're right about one thing: you'll leave now. But this time, you must take a different approach."

Michael looked up at his father, hating his judging stare and simultaneously wanting nothing more than to make this man proud. He knew, whatever his father asked of him, Michael would do it. "Tell me what to do," Michael said. "I won't miss again."

A smile spread across the Sovereign's face. "I know," he said. He stood and descended the dais. He stopped directly in front of Michael and placed a hand on his shoulder. "Let Charles enter the stronghold," the Sovereign said. "Allow him to get the second key—*if he can.* As I said, once he obtains a key he'll be transported directly outside the stronghold. But this time, you'll be waiting for him."

Michael nodded but said, "So you don't want me to enter the stronghold then?"

The Sovereign returned to his throne and crossed one leg over the other. "There are two ways to hunt," he said. "Stalk your prey or set a trap. We already know you're not so skilled at the first option."

Michael's eyes flicked away from the Sovereign's.

"So let your prey come to you," he said. "And this time, you won't be alone. This time, the plan will be foolproof."

Michael didn't miss the insult.

The Sovereign turned to the Chancellor. "Ready one hundred of my strongest Sovereign Guards and the fastest horses in Lumina. They ride within the hour."

The Sovereign returned his attention to Michael. "You're dismissed," he said.

Michael clenched his teeth. His boots squeaked against the marble floor as he turned to storm away from his father's presence. He'd never felt so humiliated in all his life. And all because of Charlie.

Michael knew that his father saw him as a failure and a fool, but in just a few days' time, Michael would be revealed as the champion and rightful heir. He'd make certain of that.

Charlie stared up at the slate-gray castlelike fortress.

The ominous structure emerged from the side of the mountain as if it had been hand-carved into the massive stone. He stifled a shiver and wrapped his cloak tightly around his shoulders, thankful the Sage had packed some warmer clothes for him and Brynn.

His breath billowed, visible in the cold mountain air. Snow crunched beneath his feet as he approached the second stronghold. He stopped as soon as he felt the thrum, then took a few steps back. Like the first stronghold, it seemed this one's effects began about a hundred yards away.

Snow-filled clouds shrouded the moon, making the perpetual nighttime world appear even darker. Torches lined the sides of the fortress, highlighting the ramparts with a haunting glow.

Charlie heard Brynn approach and turned to see her crossing the mountain plateau, leading their horse by its reins. He gave her a nod to indicate it was safe for her join him.

Brynn stopped when she reached Charlie but stayed one step back. A thick white cloak covered her head and draped her shoulders.

"You okay?" she asked.

Talli swooped down and landed beside them, his white fur nearly vanishing against the snow.

Charlie didn't answer. Instead, he stared straight

ahead at the Stronghold of Judgment, wondering what awaited him.

He glanced at his two new friends, thankful for their presence. Charlie hadn't realized just how critical their company would be on the journey.

He smiled to himself, thinking of how they'd rallied around him after he conquered the first stronghold. It wasn't until they'd fled the canyon and returned to their horse that Charlie realized just how much of his strength the first stronghold had drained. He'd crashed on their journey to the second one, spending the first full day of travel sleeping against Brynn's shoulder. Talli ensured Charlie didn't fall off the horse and woke him several times to offer food and water.

The second day, the cold had hit. Blankets of white snow covered their path up the Argia Mountain Range, which Brynn said covered nearly the entire northern landscape of Lumina. She'd insisted there was no other route they could take. They couldn't travel anywhere near the city and risk being detected. Surely every Sovereign Guard in Lumina was searching for them. Charlie hadn't argued, even after learning it would mean three full freezing days in the snow-covered mountains. Though, he did fear Michael would beat them to their destination.

Now they stood before the second stronghold. And Michael was nowhere in sight.

But for all Charlie knew, his brother was already inside waiting for him.

And Michael would do everything in his power to stop Charlie. Of that, Charlie was certain.

Charlie drew his cloak tighter. "I guess there's no point in putting it off," he said. "It's time to go, and it looks like this is the only way inside."

"Talli should go with you this time," Brynn said.

Charlie glanced at her. Her red braid peeked out from under the thick hood of her white cloak. Her foggy breath swirled in front of her face, mimicking the swirls in her cloudy eyes.

"But then you'll be out here alone," he said.

Brynn turned from him to stare at the fortress. "Better to be out here alone then in there alone," she said. She looked at him again, then smiled. She held Charlie's gaze for a long moment.

Charlie looked down at his snow-covered boots. "What about Michael?" he asked. "If he's not already in there, then he's on his way. You shouldn't be out here alone."

Brynn swung her leg up and over the horse. "Please," she said with amusement as she settled into the saddle. "He's only one boy. I've been living on my own for years now. I can handle myself. Besides, it's you he's after, not me." She pointed to the Roush. "And, who knows, you might need Talli's epic karate skills once you get in there." She flashed a grin in Talli's direction.

Clearly the two of them had discussed the Roush's fascination with martial arts while Charlie had been inside the first stronghold.

"I feel like she's mocking me," Talli said. "Is she mocking me?"

Brynn shrugged, winked at Charlie, then snapped the horse's reins and turned away from the stronghold.

"I'll stay back here," she called to Charlie. "You know, in case it explodes or something."

Charlie tried to laugh at her joke but couldn't. After his experience in the first stronghold, it didn't seem like explosions were out of the question.

"Are you ready, young Charlie?" Talli asked.

Charlie glanced down at the Roush. His bright-green eyes searched Charlie's.

"I shall stay by your side the entire time," Talli said.

The Roush's words filled Charlie with the strength he needed to take the first step. Then the next. Snow crunched beneath his feet and Talli took to the sky, flying directly beside Charlie as he approached the Stronghold of Judgment.

Then the feeling hit—the familiar pulse and thrum of the power of darkness.

Charlie glanced at Talli. It seemed the Roush felt nothing.

Chapter Seven

But for Charlie, the sensation intensified with each snowy step, filling him with more and more dread.

CHAPTER EIGHT

A GUST OF WARM AIR greeted Charlie inside the second stronghold. The towering wooden door closed behind him and Talli with a loud boom. Charlie stared straight ahead into the cursed fortress, noting the striking difference between this one and the first. Stark white walls lined with torches framed a long white marble hall. The inside of the fortress was surprisingly bright.

Charlie shrugged off his cloak. "It's much warmer in here than outside," he said to Talli, who swooped down beside him.

The Roush shook out his wings. "Is it? I hadn't noticed."

"That's because you're covered in fur," Charlie said. "You're probably always warm."

He draped his cloak over his arm and started down the hall. The pulse of the stronghold intensified with every step. Charlie leaned into it, hoping it would lead him to the key and not Michael.

"I hate him," Charlie mumbled.

"Who?" Talli asked.

"Isn't it obvious? Michael."

"Ah," the Roush said. "Then you wish him dead."

"I didn't say I wanted him dead," Charlie clarified. "I said I hate him. He's the one who's trying to kill me."

Talli took to the air. "In my world, the great mystic taught that anyone who hates a brother or sister is a murderer." He flew ahead.

A moment of guilt washed over Charlie. "I've never thought about it that way," he said to himself.

"Look at this," the Roush said, gliding to point out an alcove. A bright-white statue was situated in the center, a marble sculpture of a woman crouched beside a small child. The woman draped a motherly arm around the boy, and in her other hand she cupped a butterfly. The child gazed at the creature with wonder.

The image stirred Charlie's mind, arousing thoughts of glowing butterflies. He still hadn't seen any since entering Lumina. The statue also evoked a deep sense of longing for a tender moment like this one with a mother—a moment he'd never had. Charlie pulled his gaze from the statue and adjusted his cloak on his arm. He was sweating beneath it.

"Let's keep moving," he said to Talli. "I need to find the key and get out of here as fast as possible."

Charlie stepped away from the statue and Talli followed.

The hall seemed to widen. Now Charlie could see that alcoves with white statues lined both sides of the corridor. He observed each one as they passed.

"It's like a museum," he said, wiping sweat from his brow.

Each statue was unique, depicting ordinary scenes — like the mother and child—and other images of people Charlie could only guess were a part of Lumina's history.

A bead of sweat slipped into his eye. He tried to wipe away the salty burn.

"It's a furnace in here," Charlie said.

Talli glided beside him. "What do you mean?"

"It's hot. Really hot." Charlie felt his internal temperature rising too. "Don't you feel that?"

"I suppose the temperature does seem to have shifted in an upward motion," Talli said.

Charlie shot him a quizzical look but continued searching for any clues that he was headed toward the key. But at this point, there was only one way into the stronghold.

Charlie swallowed. His mouth was dry. Sweat poured down his back and soaked his tunic. He groaned and threw his cloak to the side of the hall.

"Why's it so hot in here?" Irritation tinted his voice. "It's hotter than the island, and that's saying something." Charlie paused and sniffed the air. "Do you smell that?"

Talli glanced at him but didn't respond.

Charlie stopped in the middle of the hallway. He furrowed his brow and shook his head. "Gross!"

"What?" Talli asked, a look of genuine confusion on his face.

"Don't you smell it?" Charlie glanced around, wondering where the stench could be coming from in this pristine, white-walled structure. He wrinkled his nose. "It's like rotten eggs or something. Tell me you smell that."

Talli landed beside Charlie and drew a deep breath through his batlike snout. "Why, yes, there is an odor in the air." He scanned Charlie with his big green eyes. "Your face suggests it's terrible."

"It *is* terrible," Charlie said.

"It's just a smell." Talli flapped his wings and continued down the hall, passing countless statues.

Charlie struggled to keep up, the heat of the building now overwhelming. He longed to strip off his shirt, but it was soaked with sweat and clung to his torso.

He tried to roll up his sleeves, but they were stuck to his arms. Charlie groaned, irritated.

Talli swooped back down to meet him once again.

"Is something the matter, young Charlie?"

"Yes!" Charlie shouted. His voice bounced off the marbled halls. "It's miserably hot in here, and"—he fought back a gag—"the smell is so bad, I'm going to puke!" Charlie pulled the collar of his drenched tunic up over his nose. "How is this not bothering you?" he demanded.

Talli landed in front of Charlie and cocked his fury head to the side. "A smell is just a smell, Charlie, and a temperature is just a temperature. They only bother you if you think they're bothersome. You only suffer something if you judge it."

"What do you mean?" Charlie asked from behind his shirt collar, noting Talli's use of the word *judge*.

"Do I recognize an intense heat in this building? Yes. And is there an odd odor that fills these halls? There is. But I don't judge them as you do. Therefore, they don't judge me back. These things you deem miserable only make you miserable if you allow them."

Charlie narrowed his eyes at the Roush, only feeling more irritated by his explanations.

Talli continued, unperturbed. "In my world, the great mystic, who is the Light of the World, teaches that it's better to bless those who persecute you and turn the other cheek. When you offer love and light to something, it blesses you in return. So I choose to follow the way of love and light, and, therefore, the fact that it's hot and smelly doesn't bother me."

"You know," Charlie said. "Brynn's right. Not much of what you say makes sense."

Talli lifted his chin and stuck his snout in the air. "My job is to be a guide. I was not told I had to make sense."

Charlie shook his head. "Let's just keep moving so we can be done with this miserable place.

"It's only miserable if you say so," Talli said.

Charlie clenched his jaw and wiped his palm across his forehead. His hand felt bumpy. He yanked it away and stared down at it.

"*What is this?*"

Red bumps lined his skin. He quickly compared it to his other smooth palm, then touched his forehead again, this time with his clean hand.

The bumps were on his forehead too.

Dread rose within him.

"What's happening to me?"

When he looked down at his hands again, the red bumps had spread and looked more like boils. They crawled up his arm, visibly appearing before his eyes. He touched his cheek, his neck. They were everywhere.

"What's happening to me?"

Talli rushed to his side and touched Charlie's arm with a wing. "Calm down, young Charlie. It's just your skin. It must be a reaction to the stronghold."

"Just my skin? Talli, they burn!"

Sweat continued to pour down Charlie's back, stinging his raw, boiled flesh.

Charlie took off in a sprint down the hall, searching until he found what he was looking for. His booted feet squeaked to a stop. A gold-framed mirror hung on the wall between two statues. Charlie approached it hesitantly, remembering his experience with mirrors in the last stronghold.

Unfortunately, this reflection was accurate and revealed red pustules all over Charlie's sweat-streaked face. He tugged down the collar of his tunic. They covered his neck and chest. Even his lips bubbled with the disfiguring cysts.

"Look at me, Talli!" Charlie shouted.

The Roush appeared in the reflection behind him.

"These are disgusting! How's this happening?"

Charlie could feel more of the pulsing, painful bumps emerging on his scalp. Growing, spreading, itching, burning.

"I need to get them off of me!"

Charlie dugs his fingernails into the skin of his arm and scraped. But the boils only became redder and more enflamed. Charlie's skin crawled as if he were covered in fire ants.

"I know you're upset, young Charlie, but try to

remember that this is the Stronghold of Judgment. Whatever you judge will judge you in return."

Charlie ignored the Roush and backed away from the mirror. "We've got to get out of here."

He turned and rushed down the corridor. Talli flew close behind.

Ahead of them, the hallway ended in another stark-white wall, and in the center of it, a door.

Charlie's feet slowed. "Oh no," he groaned.

"What is it, young Charlie?" Talli asked.

"The door," Charlie muttered. "Doors in strong-holds are bad." He stopped before it.

"They're only bad if you say so—"

"Not now, Talli!" Charlie snapped.

He regretted his tone, expecting to see a look of anger or at least hurt cross Talli's face, but the Roush's innocent, quizzical expression never changed.

Sweat poured from Charlie's forehead. Nausea from the smell overwhelmed him. He felt like he couldn't breathe in the sweltering, stinking heat.

He stared at the door. Charlie needed to get out of this room before he fainted, barfed, or turned into one large boil. The palm of his hand burned as he wrapped his fingers around the doorknob and twisted. He threw open the door, stepped across the threshold, and slammed it closed after Talli swooped through.

Cool, clear air filled his nostrils. Charlie sucked in a deep breath and dropped to his knees in relief. He held out his hands in front of him. His skin was clear. He searched his face with his fingers. His skin was smooth and completely free of the painful cysts.

"They're gone! The smell and the heat too."

"Yes, they're gone," Talli said. "But what's this?"

Charlie glanced up from his hands to take in his surroundings for the first time.

They were in a large square room. The walls were still white but constructed of painted brick. A series of black-and-white photos hung on each wall, illuminated by the torchlight. Charlie crossed the room to examine one. As he neared it, he realized they weren't photos at all but realistic oil paintings. He grazed his fingers against the textured canvas and took in the scene.

Charlie recognized the image.

It was a painting of him standing in the bathroom at Saint Francis's Boys and Girls Home. Michael stood before him, permanent marker in hand, prepared to ruin Charlie's shirt.

Charlie looked away and moved to the next painting.

Again, the scene was familiar, but this time it was a snapshot from his time before the ranch in Montana, at an old foster home, with a girl who bullied him. Charlie didn't linger.

When he reached the third painting, he saw another miserable moment from his life, when a social worker informed him that, once again, Charlie would be sent to another home because he wasn't a "good fit" for his foster family—code for "they don't like you."

"How could they all be so cruel?" he asked under his breath.

A loud sound rumbled behind him.

Charlie spun, seeing a large marble sculpture rise out of the center of the floor. Two statues appeared, frozen in motion atop a large circular platform. A hammer and chisel sat on the stand, as if the sculptor had just finished their work.

Talli appeared beside Charlie. "Is that you?" he asked, pointing to the statue of a young boy with thick curly hair. The marble child cowered, his hands near his face as if shielding it.

"Yes," Charlie said, his voice quiet and even. "That's me."

"And who's that?" Talli asked, pointing to the other statue.

Charlie scanned the marble woman beside the boy. Anger marked her severe face, and her arm was drawn back as if to strike. She held a ruler.

Charlie sighed. "That's my first foster mother."

Talli was silent as Charlie stepped closer to the carved scene.

The emotions captured on the faces of the statues were so realistic, they transported Charlie directly back into the moment.

The fear on his six-year-old face flooded his body with angst. His foster mom's stern expression filled him with anger.

"I was just a kid," Charlie said, noting how young he appeared in the carved image. "How could she be so cruel to a little kid?"

He took a step closer and peered into the frozen eyes of the first woman who'd hurt him. Well, not the first. His mother had been the first. And the pain she'd inflicted upon his life by abandoning him was only magnified in every other foster situation Charlie had ever been in.

Pressure built behind his eyes, but he couldn't look away from the frozen expression of his foster mother. He stared at her for a long second, then her eyes shifted to his.

Charlie jumped back. The statue moved, drawing back its arm even farther in preparation to strike the young boy who cowered at her feet. Six-year-old stone Charlie trembled and whimpered. The sound of his sobs sucked Charlie into the moment.

"Run!" Charlie shouted at his younger self. "Run!"

But the stone boy couldn't hear him.

Charlie scanned the room, searching for a way to help. His eyes landed on the hammer and chisel. Before he could think, Charlie's fingers wrapped around the handle of the hammer. He reared back, then swung with all his strength. The head of the hammer connected with the woman's left leg. A spiderweb crack spread across the white marble. The woman flinched, but the boy cried out in pain. Charlie spun to see an identical crack form on the child's left leg.

"Now you're really going to pay," the woman said. She swung the ruler at the marble boy's face.

Charlie reacted by swiping the hammer at her attacking hand. Her fist shattered. Her carved fingers crumbled to the floor. She gasped in pain, but the stone boy wailed. When Charlie looked at him again, his right hand was missing.

He stepped back from the stone scene, stunned.

Whatever you judge will judge you in return.

Charlie spun to look at Talli, thinking he must have spoken, but the furry white creature remained silent behind him. His face gave nothing away.

"She was cruel!" Charlie shouted at Talli, feeling the need to explain himself. "She was evil! I was just a little boy!"

Charlie turned back to the statues, swinging the

hammer as he spun. He shattered the foster mother's other arm, then took a chunk out of her leg. But the little boy's body mirrored every injury.

In attacking the foster mother, Charlie was also attacking the boy made of stone.

The statues continued to move as if they were real, the foster mother becoming more and more enraged with every blow of the hammer, the little boy crumbling to pieces.

A thought flickered through Charlie's mind.

When I hurt her, I hurt myself.

What I judge, judges me back.

His mind swirled. He let the hammer hang limp in his hands.

Talli had said the great mystic taught that it's better to bless those who persecute you. And that if he offered love and light to something, it would bless him in return.

Charlie's brain wrestled with the thoughts.

How could he bless someone who was so cruel to him?

Didn't he have a right to cause pain to someone who'd caused him pain?

But when I hurt her, I'm only hurting myself.

Charlie wavered between the two paths of thought for only a second longer before making his decision.

He swung the hammer over his shoulder, arced it over the statue of the foster mother, then brought it down onto her head.

She shattered into thousands of tiny pieces.

And so did the little boy.

They were nothing more than a pile of rubble.

Charlie stared at the mess he'd made, then noticed one chunk of marble that was still intact. It was his own eye. It stared back at him blankly, then blinked.

Charlie jumped back, horrified. He dropped the hammer.

A shattering echo bounced through the room. A crack formed at Charlie's feet and the ground began to rumble.

"What's happening?" Charlie asked.

"It seems the stronghold is judging your judgment," Talli said.

The crack on the floor raced across the marble tile and reached the nearest wall. It spiderwebbed up the brick, and the walls began to crumble, then the roof.

Chunks of stone rained down around them.

"We have to get out of here!" Talli said.

"Through the door!" Charlie pointed.

Talli swooped ahead of him, dodging a large piece of debris.

"The ceiling's going to cave!" Charlie shouted. "Go!"

"Hurry, Charlie!" the Roush shouted. "Follow me!"

Charlie fixed his eyes on his flying friend and followed his path through the collapsing room.

He reached the door a second behind Talli, wrapped his fingers around the knob and pushed through the door. When they were both on the other side, he slammed it closed.

Charlie leaned back against the closed door, then slid down to the floor. He stared into the main hallway of the stronghold. His chest heaved. He was so frazzled that he barely noticed the heat and smell were gone.

"Are you alright, young Charlie?" Talli asked, scanning him up and down with his green eyes.

Charlie shook his head. "I don't know."

"What happened in there?" Talli asked.

"You saw," Charlie said. "I broke the statues."

Talli waddled closer. "Not what happened in the room," Talli said. "What happened in here?" He tapped the side of Charlie's head with his wing.

Charlie gulped air and stared at Talli. He was an interesting creature. Infuriating at times with his cryptic answers. But Talli had a pure heart. That much was clear to Charlie.

"What did you mean when you said, 'When you offer love and light to something, it blesses you in return?'"

A smile spread across the Roush's face. "Ah, you're meditating on the words of the great mystic."

Charlie shrugged, still trying to catch his breath. "What does it mean?" he asked.

Talli stretched out his wings. "How to say this another way?" He peered up at the ceiling as if searching for the answer. "Ah, I know." He cleared his throat. "What you put in darkness calls you to that darkness. And what you bless in light fills you with light."

Charlie shook his head. "That's more confusing than what you said before."

"Let me try again," Talli said. He cleared his throat. "With the same manner you judge others, you are judged. With the same manner you bless others, you are blessed."

Charlie narrowed his eyes. "So blessing is the opposite of judging?"

"Now we're getting somewhere!" Talli said excitedly. He tapped the top of Charlie's head. "Though I must say it took you a while to get there."

"I'm still not sure I'm *there*," Charlie said. He stood.

"Well, it certainly seems better than in *there*." Talli pointed to the door. He waddled a couple steps away, then settled himself directly in front of Charlie. He reached out with both wings and touched Charlie's legs, then peered up at him with a whimsical look. Charlie smiled to himself, knowing how adorable Brynn would find Talli in that moment.

"Young Charlie?" Talli said, his voice soft and low.

"Yeah?"

"You've faced much pain for such a young boy."

Charlie blinked.

"I'm sad it brings you so much suffering," Talli said. He touched a wing to his furry chest. "Seeing the suffering of another brings me great suffering too. Especially when it's someone I particularly like."

Charlie knelt before the Roush and ruffled his fury head. "You know, you're an amazing friend, Talli."

"Of course I am," Talli said. "Why else do you think the Sage sent me?"

The Sage.

An image of the weathered man filled Charlie's mind as clearly as if he stood beside the Roush. The memory of his words returned to Charlie with a startling clarity.

The strongholds are designed to enhance the darkness within you. It's your own darkness that you will need to overcome.

The words stirred him.

You're never alone, Charlie, even in your darkest moments when you think you are. The light will always be with you because it is in you. And the light will be your greatest guide.

Charlie pondered the words for a moment, then

he said, "I'm so glad the Sage sent you. I'm grateful I'm not in this stronghold alone." Charlie stood. "Ready to keep moving?"

Talli leapt into the air and executed a spinning back kick with his short leg. He landed with a wobbly bounce but looked perfectly pleased. "Does that answer the question for you?" Talli asked with a grin.

Charlie laughed. "Yes. I think we're both ready. Let's go."

He started down the hallway that led back to the entrance, wondering where the key could possibly be.

Talli flew close behind.

"Look," Charlie pointed down the hall, noticing something different. "The stronghold changed. It's like the walls have moved or something. Do you see the—"

A loud boom echoed behind Charlie. He spun. A white wall stood directly behind him.

And Talli was gone.

CHAPTER NINE

CHARLIE POUNDED HIS FIST against the white wall. "Talli!" he shouted, then pounded harder. "Talli! Can you hear me?"

"I'm here, young Charlie." Talli's voice sounded muffled on the other side.

"Are you okay?" Charlie asked.

"Yes. I'm alright. Are you?"

Charlie stared at the barrier that separated him from his friend. "No," he said under his breath. "I'm alone. Again."

"What was that? You'll have to speak up."

"I'm fine," Charlie said louder. "But what do we do now?"

Talli was silent for a moment, then said, "I see no way to reach you on my end. Are there any openings on your side? What do you see?"

Charlie searched the wall, top to bottom and side

to side. It was as secure and sturdy as if it had always been there.

"There's nothing," Charlie said.

"What about the hallway?" Talli asked. "You were just saying that it had changed."

Charlie turned and scanned the white marble corridor. The statues that had lined the walls were gone. As was the giant wooden door that would lead to the outside.

Instead, a plain white door stood at the end of the hallway, and the alcoves where the statues once posed now formed arched openings that led into other rooms. The mirror was still there.

"The exit is gone," Charlie said loud enough for Talli to hear. Defeat filled his voice.

"You must complete your challenge," Talli said from behind the wall. "And you must continue without me. Overcome the stronghold and get the key. You can do this, young Charlie."

"What about you?" Charlie asked.

"I'll figure out something," Talli said. "I'm resourceful. And, not to worry; if I should encounter a Shataiki, I have my karate skills."

Charlie furrowed his brow. "What's a Shataiki?"

"A creature made of fear," Talli's muffled voice said.

What could that be? Charlie wondered. He glanced around but saw no creatures at all.

"Talli?" Charlie turned back and looked at the wall. He pounded on the hard surface. "Talli, are you there?"

But the Roush was gone.

Charlie sighed. "So much for not doing this alone," he muttered.

He turned and stared down the hallway once more, then took his first step.

Now alone but not overwhelmed by heat, bad smells, or boils, Charlie could truly feel the presence of the stronghold. The subtle pulse of the darkness vibrated over the surface of his skin, causing goosebumps to form. Charlie shook off a shiver and journeyed farther.

He paused a moment when he reached the first arched opening. His footfalls echoed as he entered a small square room. Another marble-carved scene sat in the center. The statues faced away from Charlie this time, but he could clearly identify them. Michael and Tyler. They stood side by side, holding something between them.

Charlie circled the marble scene, somehow knowing exactly what he'd find on the other side—himself. The image was a scene from the island, the moment Michael and Tyler had pranked Charlie by pretending to push him off a cliff. The carved image of Charlie teetered on the edge of the raised platform that held the statues, his face frozen in a look of horror. Michael and Tyler wore expressions of cruel delight.

Charlie stared at the scene for a long moment, feeling the pulse of the stronghold grow stronger with each second, pounding like his heart did as he'd dangled from that cliff.

"You've always been so horrible to me," he said to the statue of Michael. "What did I ever do to you?"

Charlie shook his head, turned, then left the room to continue down the hallway. He paused at the next opening to find a similar display, this time of another horrifying encounter with his first foster mother. Charlie didn't bother entering the room. Instead, he kept going, pausing at each arched opening to examine the painful scenes from his past. Old bullies, foster parents who'd never loved him, potential adoptions that fell through … With each passing scene, the thrum of the stronghold's darkness intensified. His judgment of those who had wronged him pulsed through his veins.

Eventually, Charlie stopped looking into the rooms and instead fixed his eyes on the white door at the end of the hall. He paused again only when he reached the gold-framed mirror. His reflection caught him off guard.

He saw his real self, not some distorted or boil-covered version of himself.

The image was genuinely Charlie.

Black curly hair, brown skin, khaki-colored tunic and pants, brown leather pouch wrapped around his waist. But his eyes seemed different. Charlie stepped closer for a better look. His golden-brown eyes seemed distant, lost. And maybe it was just the torchlight, but there seemed to be a hazy film over his pupils.

Charlie blinked and took a step back.

"What do you see?" he asked himself. Then answered his own question. "I see me. I see Charlie." His shoulders rose and fell with a deep breath. Then he repeated the words that came to him inside the first stronghold. "The light of self-love overcomes the darkness of self-hatred. This is what it means to overcome envy." He reached into the leather pouch at his waist and lightly touched the first key, allowing its presence to fill him with strength for what was ahead. He stepped closer to the mirror again, and the film on his eyes was gone. Whether it had been the lighting or the effects of the stronghold, Charlie couldn't be sure. But there was one thing he was certain of.

"It's time to get the second key," he said to himself. "It's time to overcome judgment." He paused. "Whatever that means."

Charlie backed away from the mirror and crossed the remainder of the hallway without even glancing into any of the other arched openings. He picked up his cloak when he passed it, surprised to find it still in a heap on the floor.

The echo of his steps ceased when he stopped at the white door. He pressed a hand against its smooth surface. A gentle thrum pulsed from the other side. Charlie wrapped his fingers around the doorknob. The cold metal sent a shiver through his body. He twisted and swung open the door.

A brilliant light was the first thing Charlie noticed. Hundreds of torches clung to the white walls of this circular room, making the starkness almost blinding. Charlie stepped inside, and his eyes adjusted. A dozen or so white marble statues lined the perimeter of the room, and in the center sat a gazebo.

Charlie rushed to it and took the stairs two at a time. He stood in the center of the colonnade, staring at an amber orb that hovered over an ornate pedestal. A white diamond-shaped stone sat frozen inside it.

"I did it," Charlie said. He savored the moment of his victory, noting that it didn't feel quite as spectacular as when he'd conquered the first stronghold. That didn't matter, though. What mattered was that Charlie had overcome judgment. He'd found the key.

Charlie reached a hand forward, hovered it over the amber orb, then placed it against the surface of the resin.

Nothing happened.

"Oh no." Charlie groaned. He allowed his hand to linger, hoping it was just some sort of delay. But still nothing happened. "I found the key," he said, "but I guess I haven't overcome the stronghold yet."

Charlie stepped away from the orb and turned to scan the bright room.

It was interesting, Charlie noted, that in a world filled with darkness, this stronghold could disguise itself as a place of light. Charlie knew it was anything but that. He scanned the faces of the statues, noticing they were all representations of people from his past. Specifically, they were all female, many of them mother figures.

Charlie shifted uncomfortably, feeling a familiar tangle of emotions start to unravel.

His eyes landed on the second to last statue.

It was Sarah.

Charlie descended the stairs of the gazebo and approached. Her face was frozen in the last expression he'd remembered seeing on her: eyes filled with rage, mouth open as she shouted to him down the beach, a judging finger pointed in his direction.

The moment of their fight came alive in his mind, and finally Charlie realized why he'd gotten so mad at her. Why he'd felt so much hatred toward all the people from his past represented here in this room.

Charlie felt abandoned by them.

Especially Sarah.

When she'd chosen Michael over Charlie, she touched a deep wound that had never healed.

Charlie heard a sound like stone crumbling to his right.

He turned to see a statue begin to animate.

The white marble figure approached. Charlie took a step back and scanned her head to toe. He'd never seen this woman before.

Her carved face was striking with bold features, wide eyes, and full lips. They didn't smile. Ornate braids piled atop her regal head. She carried herself like a queen draped in a flowing gown.

She continued to glide toward him, but Charlie didn't back away. He was captivated by her.

The woman paused in front of him, chin tilted down, eyes fixed on his.

And then she transformed.

White marble gave way to deep-brown skin. Black braids glimmered with metal beads. Eyes, a rich golden-brown, stared back at Charlie.

In an instant, he knew her.

"Mom?"

"Son," she said. Her voice was thick and rich, but her tone held no hint of emotion.

Charlie hesitated then asked, "Are you—are you real?"

She only said, "You don't belong here."

Her words hit Charlie like a punch to his gut.

"You should leave," she said in that monotone voice, pointing to the door.

For a moment, Charlie considered sprinting back out the door. The sight of his mother was too much. Her words crushed him like he'd crushed the statue of his first foster mother.

"Leave," his mother repeated.

All the years of Charlie's repressed grief boiled to the surface. "No," he said, his voice filled with pain. "*You* leave!" he shouted at the woman, still not sure if she was real or an apparition. The effects of the stronghold clouded his mind. "You leave!" he repeated. "Leave like you left before! You're the one who abandoned me!"

His mother didn't move.

"Why'd you do it? Why didn't you want me?" Charlie shouted. "Don't you realize what you did?" Charlie turned and scanned the room, pointing to the faces of the other statues. "Don't you know how much I've suffered because of you? Everything bad that's ever happened to me is your fault! Every single time I was rejected was because of you. Because *you* didn't want me from the start!" He stared at her again. "Mothers are supposed to protect their sons," he said, this time his voice softer. "You failed me."

His mother took a step closer, her face devoid of

emotion. Her voice was even. "Leave, Charlie. No one wants you here." She pointed to the statues.

And Charlie knew she was right.

He wasn't wanted by any of them, especially his own mother.

In that moment, he hated them. *All of them.*

And every other person he'd seen represented here in this stronghold.

What had Charlie ever done to them?

What made him so unlovable?

But Charlie reminded himself that he wasn't at fault here.

They were.

They were bad people.

Horrible people, in fact.

Cruel. Every single one of them.

Especially this woman.

"I was just a baby," he said. "I was innocent. And you threw me away like a forgotten piece of trash."

Charlie's words echoed through the marble room and returned to him with a shocking clarity.

F is for *forgotten.*

Michael's words resurfaced in Charlie's mind.

Tears pricked his eyes, but he refused to let this woman see him cry. Not after what she had done to him.

Charlie turned and started to walk away, to leave as his mother wanted him to do.

You've never been forgotten.

The voice of the Sage flickered through Charlie's mind.

I have remembered you.

Once again, an image of the man appeared in Charlie's mind. Charlie saw him as clearly as if he were here in this room.

The image gave Charlie pause. He heard the words again.

You've never been forgotten.

I have remembered you.

"But she forgot me," Charlie said.

He could still feel the presence of his mother behind him.

Even if she did, the voice of the Sage said, *would you forget her too? Would you hurt her as you believe she's hurt you?*

Charlie thought back to the first room he'd entered in this stronghold and his encounter with his foster mother.

Every time he'd hit her, he'd hurt himself.

What you put in darkness calls you to that darkness. And what you bless in light fills you with light.

Charlie dropped his head and closed his eyes. "You

don't understand," he said, not really knowing who he was speaking to. "She abandoned me. And because of her, I've been rejected over and over again. I've been alone my whole life."

Again, the familiar words of the Sage returned to him.

You're never alone, Charlie, even in your darkest moments when you think you are. The light will always be with you because it is in you. And the light will be your greatest guide.

Charlie opened his eyes and stared at his hand. When he'd overcome the first stronghold, light shone from his fingertips. But now the memory of that light felt as phony to him as this bright room in a perpetual nighttime world.

The Sage's voice spoke again. *And this world, though lost in great darkness, still has a glimmer of remembrance for the light. The light that now dwells within you. And that light is just the thing we need to save this world. The place where you do belong.*

But the choice is yours.

Charlie turned and stared at his mother. She hadn't moved. Even her expression hadn't changed.

What you put in darkness calls you to that darkness. And what you bless in light fills you with light.

Charlie took a step toward her.

"You abandoned me," Charlie said to her.

She didn't respond.

"You rejected me. And I've felt the pain of that my whole life." He sighed. "I've judged you for the decision you made to give me up. But by holding you in darkness, I've only placed myself in darkness."

Charlie pressed his lips together, still fighting back the emotion that longed to spill out.

He took another step toward her.

"But I won't hold you in that darkness anymore."

He touched her arm. "I no longer judge you. I"—he closed his eyes—"I forgive you."

Warmth filled Charlie's palm.

A soft hum filled the room.

The heat spread up his arm and flooded his body.

Charlie opened his eyes. Light seeped from his fingertips, penetrated the skin of his mother's arm, then spread throughout her body.

Light beamed from her chest, and a smile spread across her face.

This time, Charlie didn't hold back his tears. They spilled down his cheeks.

"I bless you, Mom," he said. "I bless you with light."

"Charlie," she said, her voice soft and tender. She reached out a hand and caressed his cheek. "My baby boy."

Charlie closed the distance between them, wrapping his arms around his mother in a hug he'd longed for his entire life.

As his chest connected with hers, the light that emanated from both of them collided and surged. A great gust of wind swept through the room, extinguishing every torch. But the brilliance of the true light remained, the room even brighter than before.

The hum Charlie had heard before now buzzed throughout the entire room.

He pulled away from his mom and turned to look back at the amber orb. It glowed.

"I overcame the stronghold," Charlie said.

"That you did, my son," his mother said. "You overcame darkness with light."

He looked up into her face. Tears streaked her brown cheeks. She cupped his face in her hands. "Now, it's time for you to leave," she said.

Her words hit Charlie in a fresh way. "You never wanted to send me away as a baby," he said. "But you had to. It was time for me to leave."

She nodded. "Don't you dare think that saying good-bye to you wasn't the hardest thing I've ever done. I wanted you more than life itself. I always have. I always will."

She squeezed him close again, then said, "But Charlie, it's time for you to leave."

Charlie hugged her back, then pulled away. Light still poured from his hands, from his entire body.

His mother gestured to the gazebo.

Charlie climbed the stairs, never taking his eyes off hers.

He stepped beside the orb, glanced down at the glowing amber resin, then back at his mother.

"I love you," he said.

"And I love you, baby boy," she said. "More than you could ever possibly know."

She blew him a kiss, then vaporized into light.

Fixing his eyes on the place where his mother once stood, on the place where she'd held him, Charlie pressed his palm to the surface of the amber orb.

He felt it dissolve beneath his fingers. Heard the key clink onto the pedestal.

Then, seeing the light of the room swell to a blinding brilliance, Charlie grabbed the key.

CHAPTER TEN

SARAH STARED at the other island in disbelief. Clearly it hadn't been there before. It had sprung up out of the ocean overnight.

But how was that even possible?

Raegan broke the silence that lingered over the bewildered group. "Uh, Kurtis, can you please give me a logical explanation for that?"

Kurtis shook his head. "That's impossible."

"I think it's cool!" Milo said. "I told you this island had powers."

Tyler straightened his shoulders. "Well, I vote we go over there," he said. "What if there are people who can help get us rescued?"

"Tyler," Becca said, "it's an island that appeared overnight. We're not going over there." Sarah could see Becca's tough, take-charge attitude beginning to dissolve. She had no explanation for this miraculously appearing landmass and certainly no practical solutions for how they should handle the situation. "What if it's a mirage?" Becca said.

"It's not a mirage," Tyler said. "We *all* see it. It's an island not even a half-mile away."

"Where did it come from?" Kurtis asked in disbelief.

"I'm with Tyler," Raegan said. "I think we should check it out. How do we get to it?"

"Easy," Tyler said. "We swim."

"Not all of us can swim like you."

"Then we'll build a boat," he said.

Without thinking, Sarah said, "We can't leave. Charlie and Michael are still somewhere on this island."

Tyler turned to face her. "Michael is dead. And Charlie—wherever he is—doesn't deserve to be found."

Sarah saw hatred flare in Tyler's eyes and took a step back.

"Or," Tyler said, "if you really want to, you can go get Charlie and bring him with us." He paused dramatically. "Since you know where he's hiding."

"Stop it, you two," Becca said.

"You know, technically, we wouldn't even need a boat," Kurtis said. There was an odd look of wonder on his face. "A small raft would be enough. We just need something to hold on to and keep us afloat."

"Like a boogie board?" Milo asked.

Kurtis shrugged. "Basically."

"Big enough for all of us." Raegan said.

Sarah couldn't keep her thoughts to herself any longer. "This is a terrible idea. We don't know what that island is or where it came from."

"You can stay here," Tyler said. "Maybe we don't want you on our new island anyway."

Sarah gritted her teeth and clenched her fists. "We shouldn't split up."

Tyler ignored her. "Who's coming with me? Milo? You in?"

"You know it," Milo said.

"Kurtis?" Tyler asked. "You coming?"

Kurtis glanced out across the water at the landmass. "That island sprang up overnight. I need to see this. I'm going."

Sarah folded her arms over her chest. "Well, I'm staying. I'm not leaving without Charlie and Michael."

"I'm staying with you," Maxine said.

Becca shook her head. "There's no way I'm swimming over to Mystery Island. Joey, what are you doing?"

He took a step toward her. "I'll stay."

"Fine with me," Tyler said. "You guys can stay here. The rest of us are going over there." He pointed toward the horizon, then turned to walk away. "Enjoy your island!" He called over his shoulder.

"Bye!" Sarah said sarcastically. "I hope you drown on the way over."

Maxine shot her a look. "Sarah, don't say that."

Fueled with rage, Sarah ignored her and marched toward the tree line. She would find Charlie and Michael. And she wasn't leaving the island without them.

Tyler kicked the last few feet to shore. The waves helped push the small bamboo raft onto the beach of the strange new island. It was a flat sheet, just wide enough for the four of them to hold on to while they swam, but Kurtis was right; it was all they had needed to keep them afloat over the short distance.

Following Tyler's lead, the kids climbed out of the surf and onto the sandy shore.

"Interesting," Kurtis said, flinging water from his hair.

Raegan squeezed water out of her ponytail. "What?" she asked.

"It's a real island," Kurtis said. "I half expected it to be a mirage like Becca said. What an interesting phenomenon."

"Of course it's a real island," Tyler said. "C'mon. Let's go explore."

"What exactly do you expect to find here?" Kurtis asked, following Tyler across the sand toward the trees. This beach was much wider than that of the other island, and it took them a bit to reach the foliage. The trees here looked similar yet different, the palms taller, the vegetation thicker and more colorful.

Tyler pushed his way into the jungle. "I'm hoping to find civilization and a way for us to get rescued." He led the group through the dense trees. "It would be nice to find some food, too, besides mangos and bananas."

"Like purple fruit?" Milo said from behind him.

Tyler chuckled. "Yeah, that would be nice."

"No, look."

Tyler stopped, and Milo joined him.

Milo pointed. "There's purple fruit right there."

Tyler looked in the direction Milo was pointing. The same emerald-green vines they'd seen the day before on the other island were here too, cascading over a cluster of large boulders. The deep-purple fruit peeked through the leaves.

A smile spread across Tyler's face. "C'mon," he said to Milo. "Let's get some."

Raegan was close behind.

"You guys really shouldn't eat that," Kurtis said.

Tyler reached the fruit first and snagged one off the vine. "Are you really going to listen to Bossy Becca?

C'mon, Kurtis. You're smart. Use your brain and think for yourself."

Tyler took a bite of the fruit, and Kurtis eyed him suspiciously.

Once again, the sweet flavor filled Tyler's mouth, then flooded his body. This time it tasted like blueberry cobbler. "Oh man," he groaned. "The purple fruit on this island tastes even better." The gentle pulse of energy tingled in his body. Its rhythm thrummed in his ears.

Milo dropped to the ground and leaned against one of the boulders. "It tastes like a milkshake," he said. He devoured the piece in his hand, then grabbed another.

Raegan was beside him, already on her second one.

Kurtis was hesitating. Tyler picked a piece of fruit, then approached him.

"Kurtis, you can't tell me that you're not sick of mangos and bananas." He placed the purple fruit in Kurtis's hand. "Look, nothing bad happened to the three of us yesterday. These clearly aren't poisonous."

Kurtis examined the fruit. "But you guys were acting really weird after you ate them. And what about what you did to Sarah?" Kurtis asked, sniffing the fruit.

By now, the full effects of the purple fruit flooded Tyler's body. His mind felt clearer and sharper than ever before. He felt even more connected to this island than the one they'd left.

"Let me ask you something, Kurtis," Tyler began. "Have you felt funny since arriving at that other island?"

"What do you mean?" Kurtis asked.

"Have you felt confused and maybe a little on edge?"

"My mind's felt a bit cloudy," Kurtis said. "But that's probably just from the trauma of the plane crash."

Tyler took a step closer to him. "But what if it wasn't? You know, I hate to admit it, but I think Milo has been right about that island all along. There's something unusual about it."

"Well, that's obvious," Kurtis said.

"But what if you could understand it?" Tyler asked.

"Understand the island?"

"Yeah. What if you could suddenly make sense of everything that's happened to us over the past few days? What if the island could speak to you?"

"That sounds crazy," Kurtis said. But Tyler saw the questions—and the growing hunger—in his eyes.

"Crazier than an island appearing overnight?" Tyler raised his eyebrows. "Try a bite," he said. "If you don't like it, then forget about it."

Kurtis rubbed his thumb over the fruit in his hand. "It does look good," he said.

"Trust me," Tyler said. "It's better than good."

Kurtis brought the fruit to his lips. He hesitated, then bit into the soft flesh.

Tyler saw the wave of delight hit Kurtis. His eyes widened. His pupils enlarged. A smile crept across his face, and he took another bite.

"What does it taste like?" Tyler asked.

"Carrot cake," Kurtis said through a mouthful. "But the best carrot cake I've ever had."

"Guys!" Milo ran toward them. "You're never going to believe what the island just told me."

Tyler finished his first piece of fruit. "This island or the old one?" he asked, feeling jealous that Milo had heard the voice more than once.

"This one," Milo said excitedly.

"Well, tell us," Tyler said.

"Better if I show you!" Milo had a wild look on his face.

"Let's go then," Kurtis said. He picked two more pieces of fruit before following Milo deeper into the jungle.

Tyler motioned for Raegan to come with them, and the four ventured into the forest with Milo in the lead.

Time felt distorted to Tyler. For all he knew they could have been traveling for minutes or even hours. But with every step he took, he felt the energizing pulse of the fruit overtaking his body. He felt connected to this island in an even deeper way than the last one. He hoped he'd soon hear its voice as Milo had.

"Look!" Milo shouted excitedly. "There it is! The island was right!"

Not thirty feet away, the jungle opened into a clearing. Ten thatched huts formed a circle around a smoking firepit, and in the center of it all was a long wooden table set with a lavish meal.

Raegan covered her mouth with her hand. "I can't believe it," she said.

"Whoa," Kurtis muttered.

"I was right," Tyler said to himself. A bubble of laughter welled up inside him and spilled out. "This is it!" He ran toward the little village. "We're going to get rescued!"

"Wait," Raegan called. "We don't know who these people are. We can't just barge into their village."

"Oh yes we can," Tyler said, running to the spread of food. "Oh man," he muttered. "It's like a Thanksgiving feast."

"There's no one here," Kurtis said, following Tyler into the center of the clearing. "But it looks like they'll be back soon." He stopped beside Tyler at the table. "Is that a turkey?"

Tyler nodded. "And mashed potatoes and gravy." He pointed to the wooden bowls filled with steaming food.

Milo and Raegan had joined them now.

"Macaroni and cheese," Raegan said wistfully while sniffing the air.

"And hot buttered rolls. Mmm …" Milo picked one up.

"Wait," Kurtis said. "We shouldn't eat this."

"Why?" Milo asked.

"Because we want these people to help us get rescued. We don't want to make them angry by eating all their food."

Milo looked down at the roll in his hand. A sad expression lingered on his face. "But the island told us to come here."

A thought tickled at the back of Tyler's mind, then formed into a distinct voice.

Sit and eat.

Tyler grinned. "Eat it, Milo," he said without hesitation.

It was all Milo needed to hear.

"Milo's right," Tyler said, feeling the energy of this new island pulse through his body. "The island brought us here. It wanted us to find the food."

"That's all you needed to say," Raegan said, taking a seat. Using her hand, she shoveled large scoops of macaroni and cheese into her mouth.

Tyler took a seat at the head of the table and Milo took his place at the opposite end.

Kurtis hesitated then joined them. "I guess you're

right," he said.

"It's not me who's right," Tyler said. He pulled a turkey leg from the roast, then handed the other one to Milo. "It's the island. The island is always right."

Kurtis nodded, then dove into the mashed potatoes.

Tyler took a bite from the turkey. It was the best meal he'd ever eaten.

"This is even better than purple fruit," Raegan said through a mouthful.

"Agreed," Kurtis said, now fully committed to the meal.

Tyler nodded and reached for a bread roll.

When he brought it to his lips, he caught a whiff of something rotten. He glanced around to see where it had come from.

Down the table, Milo leaned forward in his seat, hunched over the turkey leg he was devouring. "This is my favorite of the two islands," he said. Grease ran down his arm and dripped off his chin.

The image of Milo rippled like a reflection stirred in a pond. And for a second, it looked like Milo was eating a piece of rotten purple fruit, its rancid juice dripping down his face. Then, just as quickly, the image disappeared, and Milo was eating a turkey leg again.

Tyler shrugged and bit into the sweetest dinner roll he'd ever eaten.

Welcome home, Tyler. Welcome home.

The voice whispered in his mind, and for a moment Tyler wondered if he actually wanted to be rescued.

CHAPTER ELEVEN

CHARLIE OPENED HIS EYES to see the towering wooden door of the Stronghold of Judgment. He was outside the fortress.

"I did it," he said to himself, uncurling his fingers to stare at the white diamond-shaped crystal in his palm. It tingled against his skin and sent waves of energy through his arm. He brought it closer to his face. In the dim light of the torches outside the stronghold, it almost seemed to glow.

Charlie peered up at the castlelike structure. Haunting shadows slithered across the gray stone face of the building. But Charlie no longer feared the darkness of the fortress. He looked down at his palm, knowing that, though he couldn't see it now, light dwelled inside him. The light that had overcome.

Charlie drew a deep breath, allowing the moment of victory to fill and fuel him. For the first time since he'd arrived in Lumina, Charlie felt secure in his identity and confident in his mission here in this dark world. He'd already overcome two of the three strongholds. He felt unstoppable and couldn't wait to tell Brynn and Talli.

Charlie spun to search for his friends, hoping Talli had made it out safely.

He froze when he saw what was behind him. Ten yards from where Charlie stood, a person sat atop a black horse. And it wasn't Brynn.

Charlie recognized the silhouette of the figure immediately.

"Hey, Chucky." Michael swung his leg over the horse's back and dropped to the ground.

A wave of fear flooded Charlie's body. He scanned the darkness, searching for Brynn and Talli. It took his eyes a couple seconds to adjust after being in the brightly lit stronghold, but eventually the rest of the scene came into view.

One hundred yards behind Michael, an army of Sovereign Guard poised themselves with daggers drawn. They fanned out in a semicircle, covering the plateau and blocking Charlie's every exit. The guards' horses, also a hundred strong, formed a wall of sinew and muscle behind them. They snorted and stomped their hooves. Dust swirled about their powerful legs in dark, billowing clouds.

"I see you searching for an escape," Michael said from his place beside his horse. "I'll help you with that. There isn't one. We have you completely blocked in."

Charlie scanned the crowd, searching for Brynn or Talli, but neither was there. He could only hope that Brynn had hidden when Michael and his army approached. And Talli? If he was lucky, he'd found another way out of the stronghold and flown to safety.

Charlie drew a shaky breath, feeling his confidence fade.

Michael took a step toward him, hands held up in surrender. "How about we talk for a minute?" Even in the dark Charlie could see the twitch of Michael's lips. "You know, brother to brother."

Charlie took a step back. His foot hit the front step of the stronghold. There really wasn't anywhere for him to go.

"How do I know you're not going to kill me?" Charlie asked, eyes searching the background for any opportunity to escape.

"Oh, I'm going to kill you," Michael said. "Just not yet. I've got some things I'd like to say to you first." He shrugged and stepped closer. "Plus I thought I'd see if you have any final words. Perhaps a message you'd like me to take back to our father?"

Charlie noted the black and midnight blue fatigues Michael wore. An onyx-black metal breastplate covered his chest. The snow-filled clouds parted, and moonlight glittered off the armor's polished surface. Michael drew closer.

Charlie hesitated, reminding himself of the two keys in his possession. He didn't have royal armor or guards, as Michael did. But he did have something Michael wanted. Still, Charlie's nervous breath billowed in front of him. He wrapped his cloak around his shoulders, then took a step to meet his brother halfway.

It had been days since Charlie stood this close to Michael, and his appearance caught Charlie off guard. Michael's angular face looked even more harsh than Charlie remembered, his light-brown skin even paler in this darkened world. But the thing that most surprised Charlie was the subtle film that covered Michael's hazel-green eyes. Charlie doubted anyone else would notice it. To him it was a sign of Michael's surrender to the darkness.

"Michael," Charlie said, forcing his voice to be stronger than he felt.

Michael dipped his head in artificial politeness. "Charles."

Charlie shifted his shoulders back and tilted his chin up. "You said you wanted to speak to me?" He drew on every ounce of confidence and strength he'd discovered in himself over the past several days.

Michael stared at Charlie for a long moment.

"What?" Charlie asked.

Michael shifted, revealing a bow and quiver full of arrows slung over his shoulder. "Nothing," he said. "I'm just trying to see it, but I can't."

"See what?" Charlie asked.

"Any sort of family resemblance," Michael said. He sneered. "You know, twin similarities or something like that. I'm still not sure I believe it."

"Me either," Charlie said under his breath. But as he examined Michael closer, he saw a faint resemblance to the sculpture of their mother he'd encountered inside the stronghold.

"I bet no one back on the island would ever believe we're twins," Michael said.

Charlie's mind drifted to the group of children they'd left behind. "What do you think happened to them? Do you think they even realize we're missing?"

Michael's posture relaxed a bit. "I really haven't thought much about them until now." He shrugged. "But knowing the way you and I left things, they probably think I killed you." Another smile flickered across Michael's face. "And they'll be right. *Soon.*"

"But they're your family," Charlie said. "Aren't you worried about them?"

Charlie recalled something the Sage had said to

him: the outcome of Charlie's actions here in Lumina impacted the kids in the other world. But what of Michael's actions?

"They were never really my family," Michael said. "My real family is here in Lumina. This is my home now. I belong here, reigning beside my father."

"*Our* father," Charlie corrected.

"He may be your father by birth," Michael said, "but he wants nothing to do with you—just like our mother. But, unlike our mother, our father didn't abandon you because you're worthless. He disowned you because you're his enemy."

"Our mother didn't abandon us," Charlie said, drawing on the strength of her presence just moments ago.

Michael eyed Charlie suspiciously. "How do you know? Have you seen her?"

Charlie saw the questions in Michael's eyes and realized he didn't know their father was holding her captive.

Charlie's experience with their mother hadn't been a real flesh-and-blood encounter—he was aware of that. But it didn't matter. The healing of that relationship was real because Charlie's choice to bless her in light was real.

He chose his words carefully. "I had an encounter

with her," he said. "I may never know for sure why she sent us away as babies, but either way, I forgive her."

Michael's eyes narrowed. And in that moment, Charlie saw his hate-filled expression for what it really was—envy of Charlie's encounter with their mom, and a long-held judgment against her. Michael had his own darkness to overcome.

"Tell me about the Sovereign," Charlie said. He subtly scanned his surroundings, but the wall of guards was impenetrable.

Michael didn't say anything.

Charlie fixed his eyes on Michael's and took a step closer. "No, really," he said, trying to appeal to whatever humanity remained inside Michael. He fixed his mind on the two keys hidden inside his leather pouch. He could feel the gentle pulse of their strength and power— the power of the light. Charlie drew strength from it, took another step closer, then offered Michael a genuine smile. "Tell me about our father," he said.

Confusion flickered across Michael's face. He'd never seen this side of Charlie. Heck, Charlie had never seen this side of himself—it invigorated him. He touched the leather pouch at his waist, feeling the pulsing strength of the keys, then discretely removed his hand.

"What's there to tell?" Michael said. "He's only the

strongest, most powerful man that's ever existed. And he's chosen me to be his heir."

The pulse of the keys grew stronger. Charlie wondered if Michael could feel it. He didn't seem to. But Charlie knew from the way Michael looked at him that the stronghold was influencing Michael. But Charlie could also tell that, for some reason, Michael was keeping the force of the darkness in check, as if he hesitated to completely surrender.

Charlie seized the opportunity. "Are you sure you're on the right side of things here in Lumina, Michael?"

The question caught Michael off guard. "What do you mean?" he asked.

"Are you sure our father is who you think he is?"

Michael composed himself. "Of course he is," he narrowed his gaze at Charlie. "You've been talking to the Sage, haven't you? Father said that heretic would fill your mind with lies. Seems like he did. You've always been a terrible judge of character, Charlie. If you're going to question anyone's integrity, it should be the Sage's—and our mother's."

"Our mother saved us," Charlie said. "She saved us from our father. He would have killed us—both of us."

Michael scoffed. "She saved us? From what? From a kingdom where our father reigns?" Michael shook his head. "Man, the Sage really scrambled your brains. Don't you get it, Charlie? We could have been a family—a royal family. Maybe you and I would have even liked each other. We could have been real brothers, not mortal enemies. Maybe I wouldn't be standing here wanting to kill you." Michael shrugged. "But I guess we'll never know."

Charlie stared at Michael, startled by the hint of vulnerability beneath his threat. Michael *was* his brother. Suddenly, Charlie saw him in a different light. For the first time he found himself wanting to get to know Michael as the person he was, not the bully he presented himself to be. But Charlie also knew, as long as their father had an influence over Michael, that would never happen.

"I see you have another key," Michael said, shifting the conversation. "I'm surprised. I didn't think you had it in you. It's almost impressive."

Charlie touched the leather pouch.

"Is that where you keep them?" Michael asked.

Charlie didn't answer.

"Give them to me," Michael said. He took a step closer.

"I can't do that," Charlie said. He took a step back. Then another. "Come on, Michael," he said, realizing he was out of time. "Are you sure partnering with the Sovercign is the right move? You could help me save Lumina."

Michael took another step toward Charlie. "Lumina

doesn't need to be saved from anyone but you. Now give me the keys," he said through gritted teeth.

"I can't give them to you," Charlie said. "I *won't* give them to you." He inched back as he spoke. The scene felt unsettlingly familiar. Charlie's mind flashed back to the portal cave on the island, remembering how Michael had threatened him in a similar way.

"Then maybe you just need some coaxing to give up the keys," Michael said. "Perhaps the stakes aren't high enough."

Charlie stiffened. "What do you mean?"

Without taking his eyes off Charlie, Michael raised a hand and shouted loud enough for the Sovereign Guard to hear. "Bring her out!"

Charlie's stomach dropped.

Far behind Michael the army parted. Two men stepped forward, dragging Brynn between them.

"No," Charlie murmured.

He saw Brynn struggle against the guards. She put up a fight, managing to kick one of them in the shin, but their grip on her was strong.

"Run, Charlie!" she shouted. "Get out of here!"

Charlie's eyes flickered to Michael.

"Well?" Michael said. He held out his hand. "How about those keys?"

"Charlie, look!" Brynn nodded toward the stronghold.

Charlie cast a quick glance behind him. A flash of white zipped past one of the darkened windows.

"Give me the keys or you're dead," Michael growled.

"I'm dead already, aren't I?" Charlie said, inching backward again.

"Then she dies too." Michael jerked his head in Brynn's direction. "And I'll pry the keys from your cold, dead fingers."

"Go, Charlie! Run!" Brynn shouted.

Michael reached for the bow on his back.

"Charlie!" someone shouted.

Charlie spun to see the front door of the stronghold thrown open wide. Talli hovered in the air just inside. "This way!" the Roush shouted. "Hurry!"

Charlie cast a quick glance over his shoulder. Michael was frozen, his stunned eyes fixed on the strange white talking bat.

Charlie sprinted toward the front door and covered the last couple yards in a few long strides. He heard the familiar sound of an arrow being nocked and the bowstring drawn. Charlie dove through the door and slammed it closed behind him. The arrow sank into the wood with a hollow *thunk*.

Charlie didn't dare look back again.

Talli flew through the stronghold at a speed Charlie hadn't yet seen from the Roush. "This way!" Talli shouted. "I've found a way out."

Charlie pumped his legs as fast as he could. His footsteps echoed through the marble hall.

A loud boom echoed behind them, and Charlie knew that Michael had entered.

The ground rumbled and shook violently. He heard statues tumbling from their pedestals and crashing into the marble floor. One of them exploded with a shatter of stone as he ran past.

"What's happening?" Charlie shouted to Talli.

Another statue exploded. Small chunks of marble debris pelted Charlie.

"I think the stronghold is reacting to your brother," Talli called down from the air.

As if on cue, a large chunk of the ceiling crumbled and collapsed directly in Charlie's path, nearly hitting Talli on its way down.

Charlie dodged the rubble and forced his legs to move faster. "Get us out of here, Talli!"

"Through the door at the end of the hall!" Talli said. "Quickly!"

Charlie followed the Roush and yanked open the door that led to the room where he'd destroyed the statue of his foster mother and six-year-old self. The room looked exactly as he'd left it, the statues a pile of crumbled stone, and the floor, walls, and ceiling all cracked.

"There's a basement," Talli said. "The statues came up from the floor. Remember? Here. Help me." Talli landed and shoved a piece of marble out of the way, revealing a hole in the floor. "I already tried, and I can fit," Talli said. "We just need to make a space wide enough for you."

Charlie heaved the hunks of stone away until he'd cleared an opening big enough for his slim body to fit through. For the first time in his life, he was grateful to be small.

Talli dropped into the hole first. Then Charlie squeezed himself through the opening.

Chaos erupted in the hall outside the room. The floor trembled again. The pieces of marble Charlie had just moved began to shift.

"Quickly, Charlie!" Talli shouted from somewhere below. Charlie dropped into darkness.

A stack of thin crates broke his fall. He tumbled to the ground, rolled to his feet, and sprinted in the direction of Talli's voice.

"Hurry, Charlie!"

Michael's footsteps echoed above them. Charlie slowed his pace just enough to silence his footfall. When he caught up to Talli, he pressed a finger to his lips and pointed to the ceiling.

Talli nodded, understanding, then motioned for

Charlie to follow him around a corner into a different part of the basement.

Giant blocks of uncarved marble stood like soldiers against the back wall. Hundreds of blank canvases lay stacked in piles. And unwashed paint brushes and chiseling tools sat beside an old washing station in the corner.

"No time to take in the scenery," Talli whispered. He waved Charlie over to a round metal grate in the floor. "You'll need to move this."

"Where does this lead?" Charlie asked. He wrapped his fingers around the rusted metal grate, lifted, and slid the heavy covering to the side.

Talli shrugged. "All drains lead out. Right?"

It was the first time Charlie had ever seen the Roush uncertain of himself.

"You don't know where it goes?" Charlie asked.

Talli's big green eyes blinked. "Do you have a better idea?"

The sound of falling stone echoed through the basement, and Charlie realized Michael had found the opening in the floor.

"Nope," Charlie said, lowering himself into the round drain opening. It wasn't much wider than his body. He gripped the sides, glanced at Talli, then said, "See you on the other side?"

"I'll be right behind you," Talli said. "I should be able to pull the grate back over the opening.

Charlie nodded, then let go.

The drop wasn't far. He fell only a few feet before feeling his backside land against a steeply sloped pipe. He couldn't see anything in the dark tunnel, but he didn't need to. The slick pipe and flowing water flushed his body down the drain. A moment later, he heard the sound of Talli tumbling through the pipe behind him.

Charlie tried to slow his descent, but the pipe only became steeper and slicker.

After several long seconds of disorienting twists and turns, the sound of rushing water reached Charlie's ears. A moment later, a faint circle of light reached his eyes. They were nearing the end, and Charlie had no idea what to expect.

He shot out of the pipe like a cannonball, drifting through the air for only a second before gravity plunged him into water.

Charlie kicked his legs frantically and swam for the surface. Finally, his head broke through. It took him a moment to get his bearings. He was in a river of slow-moving water. He spun back, seeing the drainage pipe behind him. A flash of white shot from the end of the tube, and Talli tumbled through the air. He spread his wings and caught himself, then flapped toward the far shore. Charlie swam hard, following. A moment later, he reached the grassy riverbank.

Charlie pulled himself up out of the water, rolled onto his back, and stared up at the cloudy moonlit sky, grateful to be alive.

But Michael was still inside the stronghold, determined to kill him.

And Brynn was in terrible trouble.

CHAPTER TWELVE

TALLI WADDLED UP to Charlie, shaking the water from his fur. "Well, that was fun," he said.

Charlie rolled to the side and stared at the soaking wet creature. "It's a good thing you're always right," he said. "All drains lead out."

Talli used his wings to smooth out his fur. "Of course I'm right. I'm a guide after all."

"Right," Charlie said under his breath. The weight of his mission settled over him. He stared up at the backside of the stronghold. From this side of the mountain, no one would ever know it was there. The only thing on the giant cliff that gave it away was the drainage pipe that protruded from the towering stone. Water poured from the tube and cascaded down into the river. Charlie blinked against his dark surroundings and tried to see where the body of water led.

"So what do we do now?" he asked. "They have Brynn!"

"First things first." Talli pointed to a dense forest of pines that lined the river just a few feet behind them. "We need to get out of sight. Your brother could discover the drain too. We don't want to be here waiting for him if he does."

Charlie rose to his feet and followed Talli into the wooded area. They followed the natural curve of the riverbank, using the pines and darkness as cover. A couple minutes later, they came around the bend and out the other side of the trees to find a small harbor with several boats. The river stretched into the distance. Icy wind whipped its choppy surface. There were no people that he could see. It was still night, though, it was always night here.

"You must be freezing," Talli said.

Charlie glanced down at his soaking wet clothes. Snow surrounded his booted feet. He hadn't even registered the cold until Talli brought it to his attention. Now, a deep chill settled into his bones.

"Come," Talli said and flew to the dock. He waddled onto the deck of a large sailboat.

Charlie followed as fast as he could, his movements now slowed by the cold quickly setting in. He stepped aboard the vessel and followed Talli below deck into the cabin. The Roush started rummaging through the captain's belongings.

"Ah yes," he said. "Plenty of dry clothes. Oh, and blankets too. Here." He thrust a stack of dry garments into Charlie's arms. "You must get out of those wet clothes immediately. I'll be outside waiting for you."

Charlie changed as quickly as his numb fingers would allow, dressing in a thick gray tunic and matching pair of pants. The clothes were big on him, but not too baggy once he rolled up the pants and sleeves. He found a dry cloak, wrapped it around his shoulders, then shoved his feet into a thick pair of wool socks. He layered on a second pair for good measure.

A sudden wave of panic washed over Charlie as he remembered the keys and his map. He knew the map would be wet, but he hoped the keys hadn't fallen out during his dark waterslide journey. His frozen fingers fumbled with the buckle on his leather pouch. He flipped it open. The blue and white diamond-shaped stones winked at him in the dim moonlight that streamed into the boat's cabin window. He yanked out the map and quickly unfolded it. Fortunately, the waxy coating had persevered the ink, but it would still need to dry. Just like Charlie—and his boots. He carried his soaked shoes, a blanket, and the map up to the top deck to meet Talli.

"Better?" the Roush asked.

"I'm dry, if that's what you mean." Charlie stared

at the dimly lit harbor. Two other boats were docked nearby: a smaller sailboat and a fishing rowboat. "But they have Brynn."

"Yes, I saw when I peered through the stronghold's window. I believe she saw me too."

"We have to go back for her," Charlie said.

Talli took the blanket from Charlie's arms and wrapped it around him. "No, Charlie," Talli said softly. "I will go back for Brynn. You must go after the third key."

"What? No!" Charlie's teeth chattered around his words. He fought back a shiver. "We'll go back for her together. Then the three of us can go after the key."

Talli shook his head. "Charlie, this is *your* mission. You can't abandon it now."

"But what about Brynn?"

"Brynn isn't your mission," Talli said. "But saving her can be mine."

"What about me, then?" Charlie asked. "You want me to go to the third stronghold alone?"

"You won't be alone," Talli said. "Surely you realize that by now."

Charlie looked down at his socked feet. "You're talking about the Sage?" He thought back to his experience inside the last stronghold. "It was like he was in there with me, like I could hear his voice."

"Yes, the Sage," Talli said, "but also me. I'm always with you, young Charlie. If not in body, then always in spirit."

Charlie peered up into Talli's big green eyes. "But you're my guide. You said, 'Some heroes are so great, they need more than one sidekick.' Now I don't have any."

Talli cocked his fury head to the side and smiled. "Yes—*great* heroes—but the *best* heroes are the ones who realize the sidekicks were only there to help them recognize the greatness inside them all along."

The Roush's words stirred Charlie's heart to remember something else Talli had said. Charlie recited the phrase he now understood: "Instead of changing into someone different, you could choose to become the person you've always been but didn't realize you were."

"Exactly," Talli said with a smile. "You're so close, Charlie. You already have two keys. Michael knows you need to get to the third stronghold. Surely, he will waste no time in reaching it before you. And you no longer have a horse. You must leave immediately."

Charlie wrapped the cloak and blanket tighter around his body. He already felt warmer. "And how do you suppose I'll even get to the third stronghold without a horse?" Charlie asked.

Talli made a showy gesture at the sailboat.

"I can't sail," Charlie said.

"That one then." Talli pointed to the rowboat.

"I can't just leave with some fisherman's boat and clothes," Charlie argued.

"Not just anyone's," Talli said. He pointed to a crest on the side of the boat. Charlie hadn't noticed it before. It was the Sovereign's crest.

"Look here." Talli stepped aside to reveal a small leather satchel beside him on the deck. "While you were changing, I went into the cabin of the other sailboat and gathered some provisions—water, food, even a pair of boots that look close to your size. You see. You're ready!"

Charlie stared out at the choppy waters, then looked back at the small rowboat. "I don't feel ready."

"You may not feel ready," Talli said. "But you'll surely realize that you are."

Charlie tilted his head to the side.

"What? Am I not making sense again?" Talli asked with a smile. He cleared his throat. "You are *becoming*, Charlie. You're becoming everything you hope to be, which is everything you already are."

Charlie stared at his furry friend for a long moment, then picked up the satchel, removed the boots, and laced them onto his feet.

Talli watched him with a smile.

Charlie shouldered the bag and made his way from the deck of the sailboat to the much smaller rowboat down the dock.

The boat dipped side to side as he climbed in and took a seat. Talli took to the air and hovered above him as Charlie laid the damp map across his lap.

"There's the third stronghold," Talli said excitedly.

"Yes, but here's where we are now," Charlie said, pointing. "Look how far I have to travel."

"Did you expect the journey to get easier as you went?" Talli asked. "You'll have to travel south on the river as far as you can, then make the rest of the journey by foot through the forest."

Charlie drew a deep breath, set the map aside, then gripped the handles of the oars.

Talli landed on the dock, untied the mooring rope, then karate kicked the side of the rowboat to push it out into the water.

Charlie fought back a grin and watched the Roush take to the cold Lumina sky once again. The clouds parted as he made his ascent. Moonlight outlined his silhouette in thin lines of silver.

"Farwell, young Charlie!" Talli called down to him. "Until we meet again."

Charlie pulled hard against the oars. The rowboat bounced against the choppy water.

"See you soon!" Charlie called back.

He fixed his eyes on Talli, watching the Roush until he was a mere speck against the darkened sky. He hoped *soon* would come quickly.

Another dense line of snow-filled clouds rolled over the land, blotting out most of the moonlight and the last sight of Talli.

And then, Charlie was alone.

CHAPTER THIRTEEN

I'M WORRIED ABOUT YOU," Maxine said to Sarah as the two of them exited the woods and made their way down the beach toward their camp. They'd been searching for hours, but there was still no sign of Charlie or Michael.

"Why are you worried about me?" Sarah's posture was rigid, her steps determined.

"You've been acting strange," Maxine said, "especially toward Tyler."

Sarah snapped her head in Maxine's direction. "He's the one acting strange." Sarah's words came out harsher than she intended. "Sorry." She softened her tone. "He's really getting under my skin. And I can't understand why he's so convinced that Charlie hurt Michael and I had something to do with it."

"He thinks you guys killed him," Maxine said. Her voice was quiet.

Sarah stopped and grabbed Maxine by the shoulders. She turned the girl to face her. "And you know that's not true, right?"

Maxine nodded, but tears welled in her eyes. "I know you and Charlie would never hurt Michael, but …"

"But what?" Sarah asked.

"I'm starting to worry that you and Tyler might hurt each other. I mean, he attacked you."

"Yes," Sarah said nodding. "He attacked *me*." She emphasized each word. "Tyler is the one who's losing it, Maxine, not me."

The girl looked away. "I think everyone's starting to lose it," she said.

Sarah sighed. She hated to admit it, but Maxine was right. After four full days of being stranded, people and supplies going missing, and the plane vanishing, these strange events were taking a toll on everyone.

And then there was the frightening and completely out-of-character behavior of Tyler, Milo, and Raegan yesterday afternoon. There was something wrong with that purple fruit.

"There's something wrong with this whole island," Sarah whispered to herself.

"What'd you say?" Maxine asked.

"Nothing," Sarah said.

She turned and looked out across the water at the

mysterious new landmass that had appeared overnight. From where Sarah stood, she could see the bamboo raft Tyler and his crew had used to swim across the ocean. It sat abandoned on the beach, and the kids were nowhere in sight.

Maxine cleared her throat. "But you said you hoped Tyler would drown on the way over to the other island."

Sarah sighed. "I didn't mean it, Max. I was angry with him. Sometimes we do and say things when we're angry that we don't really mean."

But deep down, Sarah wondered if she was being honest with Maxine—and herself. Because to some degree, Maxine was right. Sarah *was* losing it. The longer she was on this island, the more clouded her head felt—with fear, uncertainty, and whenever Tyler was around, a hot, nearly uncontrollable rage.

"Can't you just forgive him?" Maxine asked. Innocence filled her nine-year-old voice.

Sarah noted the way Maxine looked at her. She could tell that Maxine loved both Sarah and Tyler equally, as if they were her own flesh and blood sister and brother, and all she wanted was for her family to get along.

Sarah drew a deep breath. "For you, Maxine, I'll try."

Maxine nodded, seeming satisfied with Sarah's response.

"Oh hey," Sarah said. "I have something I've been

meaning to show you." She pulled the water bottle out of her pocket and held it out for Maxine to see the cocoon inside.

A smile appeared on Maxine's face. She took the bottle from Sarah's hands and examined the chrysalis. "Is it glowing?" she asked.

"I think so," Sarah said. "It's hard to tell, but, yeah, I think it's glowing."

"Like Charlie's butterflies." Wonder filled Maxine's voice. "That's cool. Did you show Kurtis?" she asked. "I wonder what kind of caterpillar it is."

Sarah took the water bottle back from Maxine. "No, I didn't show him. I haven't shown it to anybody but you."

"Why?" Maxine asked. "Kurtis said there are no other insects on the island. He'd probably like to see it."

"Maybe," Sarah said, her voice dropping. "But it feels too important to share, like a secret or something." She held the bottle up to her face and stared at the glowing cocoon. "And, I don't know," she shrugged, "it sounds silly, but this cocoon gives me hope."

Maxine watched her for a minute before saying, "Isn't hope something you *should* share?"

Sarah considered Maxine's words, then returned the bottle to the pocket of her skort. Instead of answering Maxine's question, Sarah said, "I'm really glad you're here with me, Maxine."

Maxine's eyes lit up with her full smile. "Me too," she said.

They crossed the vacant beach to the rocky overhang they'd turned into their camp. Becca approached, wearing an expression of uncertainty.

"What's wrong?" Sarah asked.

Becca kept her voice low. "Joey and I were just standing here, keeping the fire going, when we thought we heard voices coming from the woods." Becca pointed to the jungle that stretched behind their camp.

"Voices?" Sarah asked. "Really?"

Becca nodded. "I think someone came to rescue us."

"Why didn't you go see?" Sarah asked. "What are we waiting for? Let's go."

Becca shook her head. "What if there *are* other people who live on the island?" She paused. A look of terror flashed across her face. "And what if they're hostile?"

Sarah could tell that Becca's imagination was spiraling.

"There's only two options for who it could be," Becca said. "Either we're being rescued or we're about to be ambushed." Her voice sounded strained.

Joey stood beside her, nodding, but he said nothing.

Sarah stared at the tree line for only a second before marching toward it.

"Where are you going?" Becca demanded.

Sarah touched the pocket of her skort where she kept the cocoon. "I'm choosing to have hope," she said. "There's always a third option. Now are you coming with me or not?"

"I'm coming," Maxine said and rushed to catch up.

"Good," Sarah said. "Joey? You coming?"

He nodded and followed.

Sarah glanced over her shoulder. "Becca, we're better off sticking together."

Becca glanced at the other island across the water. "Fine," she said. "I'm coming."

The four kids pushed through the thick vegetation.

Becca stepped up beside Sarah. "Shhh … Did you hear that?"

Sarah stopped and listened. "Oh my gosh, you're right. I heard it. There is someone here."

"It sounded like the voices came from this direction," Becca said, and pointed.

They quickened their pace.

Laughter drifted through the trees. The voices grew louder.

"Look," Sarah said, pointing up ahead.

They'd only traveled a minute or two into the wooded part of the island when Sarah saw the backside of what looked to be a small clearing. Large boulders surrounded its perimeter, each one about six feet tall and just as wide. They were arranged in a circle, and it sounded like the voices came from the center.

Sarah froze and motioned for the others to stop. She couldn't see past the large boulders.

"What is it?" Becca whispered.

Sarah tilted her head to the side, thinking. "I've been through this part of the island countless times," she said. "I've never seen these rocks before. Have you?"

"Maybe," Becca said. "I don't know."

"I think we'd remember this," Sarah said. Despite the heat of the day, a chill ran through her body. Sarah shivered. "This island gets weirder by the minute."

Laughter erupted from the other side of the boulders, and Sarah motioned for everyone to follow her silently. She peered around the side of one of the giant rocks to see a circle of ten massive stones. A fallen tree stretched along the ground across the diameter, and seated around it were Tyler, Milo, Raegan, and Kurtis. They hunched over the tree and appeared to be eating something.

Furrowing her brow, Sarah stepped around the rock and entered the clearing. The other kids didn't even notice her. As Sarah approached, a putrid, rotting smell pierced her nostrils. She scrunched her nose and glanced around to see what was causing the stench. That's when she noticed the heaps of rotting purple fruit in front of each of the kids seated around the log.

Brown spots covered the once vibrant purple flesh

of the fruit, and yellowish pus oozed from each piece. Milo lifted a piece to his mouth, and sticky goo ran down his chin. The sour smell made Sarah gag. She covered her nose with her hand and stepped toward the group. Maxine, Becca, and Joey joined her.

"Gross," Maxine said.

Tyler turned toward her. "Hey," he said. "How'd you guys get here?"

Sarah shook her head. "I was about to ask you the same thing. When did you get back?" She noted the way Kurtis huddled over his pile of rotting fruit. He shoveled handfuls into his mouth without looking up at them.

"And what on earth are you doing?" Sarah asked, swallowing the bile that crept up the back of her throat. The smell was nauseating.

Tyler stood and wiped rancid juice from his mouth with the back of his forearm. His pupils were bigger than usual. "What are you doing on our island?" Tyler asked.

Sarah narrowed her eyes and shook her head. "What are you talking about? You're on *our* island— the original island."

Tyler's expression wavered between anger and confusion.

"When did you get back?" Becca asked. "I should have seen you. I was at the camp the whole time."

"And the raft is still on the beach on the other island," Maxine said.

Milo and Raegan had stopped eating and were paying attention to the conversation. Kurtis was the only one who continued to stuff his mouth with the decaying purple fruit.

"Something isn't right here," Sarah said. "You guys are confused, and probably because you're eating purple fruit—rotten fruit at that. We told you to stay away from this stuff."

Tyler stormed over to Sarah and got right in her face. The stench of rot from his mouth was so intense, she had to hold her breath. "No, you're the one who's confused," Tyler said. "This is *our* island and *our* village and *our* food."

Sarah felt heat rise within her. "What are you talking about? You're not making any sense!"

Milo joined in. "This is *our* table!" He pointed at the fallen tree. "And *our* Thanksgiving feast."

Sarah's eyebrows pulled together. "That's rotten fruit, Milo. You can't see that?"

He ignored the question. "And this is *our* village. This hut is mine," he said, pointing to a boulder. "And this one is Raegan's, and the biggest one is Tyler's," he said, indicating the biggest of the stones. "And Kurtis hasn't picked his yet because he can't stop stuffing his face with mashed potatoes."

"I'm so confused," Joey said.

"No, Joey," Sarah said to him, "*they* are the ones who are confused. And it's because they're eating this purple fruit. Tyler, look at me!" Sarah demanded. "*You are on the original island.*" She enunciated each word. "And I can prove it to you."

"No," he said. "You're on *our* island, and I can prove it to you."

Sarah took a step back from him. The same intensity she saw on Tyler's face yesterday had returned. Hatred flared in his eyes, and Sarah found herself afraid to stand too close to him.

"Let's see who's right then," Sarah said.

Tyler folded his arms over his chest. "Fine."

Sarah led the way. "Follow me."

The other seven children followed Sarah back to the beach. They covered the short distance in under two minutes and emerged on the familiar stretch of sand with the rocky overhang that protected their camp.

Sarah pointed to the ocean. "There's *your* island," she said in a mocking tone. "With *your* raft that *you* insisted upon making. I don't have any idea how you guys made it back, but here you are."

"I don't feel so good," Kurtis said. "Those mashed potatoes must have been bad." Kurtis covered his mouth and doubled over, then he ran a short distance away and vomited up purple bile.

"See," Sarah said. "Purple. It's all purple. There were *no* mashed potatoes and *no* Thanksgiving feast."

"Oh, no," Raegan said in shaky voice. "Seeing people puke makes me puke." She rushed back toward the trees and hurled purple chunks.

Tyler shook his head. "No! You're lying, Sarah! You're trying to trick us!"

"Yeah," Milo chimed in. "The island told me! You're liars and thieves!"

"Thieves?" Sarah threw her hands into the air. "Nothing you guys say makes any sense!"

"You stole the supplies and our food from the beach," Milo said. "You're trying to keep it all to yourselves."

Sarah took a step forward. "Milo, you sound insane."

"Don't listen to a word they say, Milo." The sound of Tyler's voice chilled Sarah. "You're right; they *are* liars and thieves." He paused. "*And murderers.*"

Sarah's simmering frustration with Tyler boiled over. "I've had it with you!" she shouted.

"And I've had it with you!" Tyler shoved her.

Sarah pushed him back with a strength she didn't realize she had.

Tyler stumbled and nearly fell.

"Stop!" Maxine shouted. "Don't do this!"

A dark looked crossed Tyler's face. He rushed Sarah. The entire weight of his body collided into hers.

Sarah landed hard on her back. Wind knocked out of her, she stumbled to her feet.

Tyler threw a fistful of sand into her face.

Sarah screamed. Tears welled in her eyes, burning against the scratchy grains. She blinked, unable to see.

Tyler's laughter rang in her ears.

Sarah wiped at her eyes until they cleared. Her mind was clouded with rage now. She didn't think, just reacted. Her hands searched the ground until they landed on a fist-sized stone. Fingers locked around it, she stood, crossed the short distance between her and Tyler, then reared back with the rock in her hand. She aimed to smash it into the side of Tyler's face, but he moved at the last second. The rock fell to the ground. Bright-red blood streamed from a cut on his temple where the rock had grazed him. The blood dripped down his cheek and off his chin.

Sarah could hear nothing but Tyler's furious screams. The rest of the kids and their protests faded from her awareness.

Sarah stooped to retrieve the rock. This time, she wouldn't miss.

She flicked her eyes away for only a second. When she saw him again, Tyler had a baseball-bat-sized piece of driftwood in his hands. He reared back to swing at Sarah.

Maxine stepped between them. "Stop—"

The word was cut short, punctuated by the sound of wood cracking against Maxine's tender skull.

The girl dropped to the sand, her head hitting Sarah's abandoned stone as she fell.

Silence shattered the chaos.

No one moved.

Maxine's body was still. Crimson red soaked the sand beneath her head.

Sarah dropped to her knees, her mind spinning and now suddenly clear. "Maxine!" She shook the girl's shoulders. "Maxine!"

The girl's eyes were open, her face frozen in an expression of concern for her friends.

But she didn't move.

Didn't breathe.

"Maxine." Sobs choked Sarah's voice as she spoke the young girl's name.

Sarah looked up at the rest of the kids, who stood in a circle around her. She cradled Maxine's limp body to her chest. Tears spilled down her cheeks.

Tyler hovered above her, his eyes now clear. His face twisted with an expression of horror.

Sarah looked up at him, tears blurring her vision. "What have you done?" Her words sounded too loud on the still beach.

"It was an accident," Tyler said. "I didn't mean to. She stepped in the way." His voice became frantic. "Why did she step in the way?"

The other kids stared at him, but no one spoke a word.

Tyler wavered on his feet. "Is she—"

"Yes, Tyler!" Sarah shouted through sobs. "Maxine is dead!"

Tyler took a step back from the group. Then another.

He registered the eyes of his peers staring at him, some filled with tears, others frozen in shock.

"It was Sarah's fault!" Tyler said, pointing a finger at Sarah. "She made me do it! She started it!"

No one said a word.

Tyler backed away. "She got Maxine killed just like she got Michael killed."

Sarah clung tighter to Maxine's body. She shook her head. Tears spilled down her face. "How could you say that?" she asked.

But inside, Sarah wondered if Tyler was right.

Her mind couldn't process that reality—not now. Not with the shock and grief so raw.

"How could you say that?" Sarah screamed at him again, this time feeling her voice crack.

Waves of emotion mingled on Tyler's face. "*You* did this to her," he said to Sarah in a low voice. "And if I ever see you again, I'm going to kill you." He looked away from her toward the woods. "Milo, Raegan, Kurtis, let's go."

The three kids' expressions said they didn't know what to do. So they followed Tyler's orders and moved toward the tree line with him.

"*You* stay on the beach," Tyler said. He pointed a finger at Sarah. She saw the tremor in his hand. "The village is mine. If any of you cross into it, I'll kill you." He turned without another word and rushed back into the woods with Milo, Raegan, and Kurtis close behind.

Sarah shook her head. Even now, Tyler was lost in his delirium. Remembering one of the last things Maxine said to her, Sarah wondered if she was too.

Becca and Joey knelt beside her and wept, each of them clinging to the tiny body of the sister they loved. She felt so frail in Sarah's arms, so broken, and no longer filled with hope.

Sarah buried her face against Maxine's chest and wailed, realizing that she, too, no longer had any hope.

Continued in Book Three:

Redemption